Nobody tried to figure out anymore how Angeline knew all the stuff she knew, the stuff she knew before she was born. Instead, they called her a name. They called her "a genius." And even though it really didn't explain anything, everybody considered it a satisfactory explanation. Like the way she always knew what tomorrow's weather would be. "How does she do it?" someone might ask. "She's a genius" they'd be told, and somehow that would explain it. And that way, nobody ever had to really try to understand.

# SOMEDAY ANGELINE

# LOUIS SACHAR

# SOMEDAY ANGELINE

**BLOOMSBURY**

LONDON  NEW DELHI  NEW YORK  SYDNEY

Bloomsbury Publishing, London, New Delhi, New York and Sydney

First published in Great Britain in 2007 by Bloomsbury Publishing Plc
50 Bedford Square, London WC1B 3DP

Published by arrangement with HarperCollins Children's Books,
a division of HarperCollins Publishers.

A CIP catalogue record for this book is available from the British Library

ISBN 978 0 7475 8723 1

Typeset by Dorchester Typesetting Group Ltd
Printed and bound in Great Britain by CPI Group (UK) Ltd, Croydon CR0 4YY

10

www.bloomsbury.com

*Someday Angeline*, a good story
with lots of funny jokes,
is dedicated to everyone who can
tell whether or not a book is any good—
by smelling it.

SOMEDAY
ANGELINE

# Nina's Untrained Ear

"Octopus," said Angeline Persopolis.

She was only a baby. It was the first word she ever said, which was why it was preposterous.

Nina, Angeline's mother, was the one who had heard it. Her big eyes opened even wider. "Abel!" she screamed with delight. "Abel! Angeline said something. She said her first word! Abel!"

"Wha'd she say?" asked Angeline's father as he rushed into the living room, where Angeline lay in her crib.

Nina suddenly looked very confused.

"Come on, Nina," urged Abel, "what did she say?"

Nina looked oddly at her husband. "She said . . . *octopus*?"

"Octopus?" questioned Abel.

They turned and looked at Angeline, who lay peacefully sucking her thumb.

Abel called the doctor because, well, he didn't know what else to do. It was she, the doctor, who said it was "preposterous." She told them that they had absolutely nothing to worry about. She said that Angeline was only making simple baby noises—"ock" and "tuh" and "puss"—and that it was just a coincidence that it had happened to sound like "octopus" to Nina's untrained ear.

Angeline's parents were satisfied. They realized it had to be a coincidence because, after all, Angeline had never seen an octopus, and they couldn't remember ever saying "octopus" in front of her. In fact, they couldn't remember ever saying "octopus" at all.

Okay, fine. However, to this day Angeline remembers saying "octopus." She is eight years old now. She has big green eyes like her mother's and jet black hair like her father's. And she remembers lying in her crib, in her soft pink blankets, peacefully thinking about the ocean, and the fishes, and especially about the funny-looking creature with eight legs.

There are some things you know before you are born. As Angeline grew up she seemed to know a lot of things that couldn't be explained any other way.

When she was three, her mother, Nina Sandford Persopolis, died.

And then again, there are some things you never know.

# ONE
# How Abel Smells

Angeline lay on the floor of the living room with her feet up on the sofa, reading a book. The living room was also her bedroom. The sofa folded out into a bed.

It was a book about a sailor who was in love with a beautiful lady who didn't love him back, which was why he became a sailor—to forget her. Only he couldn't forget her, but he was an excellent sailor and he fought a pirate with one eye.

Nobody tried to figure out anymore how Angeline knew all the stuff she knew, the stuff she knew before she was born. Instead, they called her a name. They called her "a genius." And even though it really didn't explain anything, everybody considered it a satisfactory explanation. Like the way she always knew what tomorrow's weather would be. "How does she do it?" someone might ask. "She's a genius" they'd be told, and somehow that would explain it. And that way, nobody ever had to really try to understand.

She heard her father outside the apartment door. She bent the page in her book to mark her place and jumped up to greet him as he opened it.

"Don't hug me until I take a shower," he said, pushing her away. "I smell like garbage."

"I like the way you smell," said Angeline.

"You like the smell of garbage?" asked Abel.

"I do," said Angeline.

She watched him walk into the bathroom and almost immediately she heard the shower running. "I bet he can take off his clothes faster than anyone in the world!" she thought.

He worked for the sanitation department. He drove a garbage truck.

In an odd way, he was afraid of Angeline. He remembered the time they went into a music store where she sat down and played the piano without ever having had a lesson. Everybody in the store stopped and listened to her. It was so pretty it scared him. He hadn't taken her back there since.

More likely, he wasn't as afraid of her as he was afraid of himself. He was afraid he was going to somehow blow it for her. "How's an idiot like me supposed to raise a genius?" he often wondered. Probably if they didn't call her that name, a genius, he wouldn't have been half as scared.

He put on his pajamas and robe. It wasn't even six o'clock but he was already dressed for bed. He never went out at night. He hadn't gone out for over five years, not since Nina died. He stepped into the living room. "Now you can hug me," he said.

Angeline hugged and kissed her father. "I liked the way you smelled before better," she told him.

She followed him into the kitchen and watched him cook dinner. "Tomorrow, will you take me on the garbage truck with you?" she asked.

He sighed. "No," he said firmly. "You know you don't belong on a garbage truck. Besides, you have school tomorrow."

"I hate school," said Angeline.

"Why does she always want to ride on that filthy truck?" Abel wondered. He hated the garbage truck. The only reason he still worked at that stinking job was for Angeline, so that he could make enough money to send her to college someday. Someday buy her a piano. Buy her nice clothes because someday she was going to be a famous scientist, or a concert pianist, or President of the United States. "Someday, Angeline . . ." he thought.

"Well then, how about on a holiday when school's closed?" she asked. "Then can I ride in the garbage truck?"

"Someday, Angeline," he said.

# TWO
# A Goat with Two Heads

Angeline was put in the sixth grade. They put her there because, well, they had to put her somewhere and they didn't know where else to put her. They put her in Mrs. Hardlick's class and that was probably the worst place to be put. She sat at the back of the room.

She started to put her thumb in her mouth but caught herself. She was smart enough for the sixth grade. She was the smartest person in the class, but she still did dumb things like suck her thumb. She knew Mrs. Hardlick hated it when she sucked her thumb. Sixth-graders are not supposed to suck their thumbs. She also cried too much for the sixth grade.

"Who was Christopher Columbus?" Mrs. Hardlick asked the class.

Angeline was the only one who raised her hand.

Mrs. Hardlick looked annoyed. "Somebody else this time," she said and glared at Angeline. "It's always the same people."

Angeline lowered her hand. It wasn't her fault she was the only one. She didn't think Mrs. Hardlick should have been mad at *her* for raising *her* hand. It was everybody else's fault for not raising theirs. But in her mind she could hear Mrs. Hardlick saying sarcastically, "It's always everybody else's fault, never your own." As she thought this, her thumb slipped into her mouth.

Mrs. Hardlick told the class about Columbus. She said that Columbus discovered America.

Angeline knew that was wrong. How could Columbus have discovered America when there were already lots of people here when he arrived? She knew that America was actually first discovered by the first snail to crawl out of water and onto land. It was something she knew before she was born.

However, she tried to give both Mrs. Hardlick

and Mr. Columbus the benefit of the doubt. "Maybe," she thought, "*from his own point of view* Columbus discovered America." But that didn't seem true either because even after Columbus got here, he still didn't know he was in America. He thought he was in India, which was why he called Americans "Indians."

Mrs. Hardlick said that Columbus proved the world was round.

Angeline knew that was also wrong. If he really had made it to India, *then* he would have proved it was round because India was east and he sailed west. But he bumped into America first and he could have sailed to America even if the world was flat.

Besides, everybody knows the world is round before they are born. That's why nobody is even slightly surprised when they first learn it in school.

These were the thoughts occupying Angeline's mind when Mrs. Hardlick suddenly called her name. "Angeline!" she commanded. "Take your thumb out of your mouth right now!"

"Oops," she thought as she quickly pulled it out.

"We don't suck our thumbs in the sixth

grade," said Mrs. Hardlick proudly.

She heard some of the other sixth-graders snicker.

Mrs. Hardlick resented Angeline. She didn't like having an eight-year-old kid in her class of sixth-graders. She especially didn't like having an eight-year-old kid who was smarter than she, although Mrs. Hardlick would never admit that Angeline was smart. In Mrs. Hardlick's mind, Angeline was a genius, which had nothing to do with being smart. It was more like being a freak, like a goat with two heads.

"Only babies suck their thumbs," said Mrs. Hardlick.

Angeline felt ashamed. Even kids in the third grade, her age, didn't suck their thumbs anymore. She felt like she was going to cry. "Oh, come on, Angeline," she told herself. "Don't start crying. Not now!" She cried way too much for the sixth grade. She even cried a lot for the first grade.

"Look, she's crying," someone teased.

She was not. It wasn't true. But then, as soon as she heard that person say it, then, wouldn't you know it, she did start to cry.

"She may be smart but she's still a baby," said someone else.

"She's not smart, she's a freak."

"Angeline, don't be a crybaby," Mrs. Hardlick admonished her. "If you feel you must cry, go outside. You may come back in when you are ready to act like a sixth-grader."

Still crying, Angeline walked outside.

"What a freak," she heard someone say.

She sat down outside, next to the door. She was wrong. Mrs. Hardlick didn't hate it when she sucked her thumb. It was just the opposite. Mrs. Hardlick loved it. The whole class loved it. They loved to put her down. And whether she realized it or not, that was why she cried. It wasn't because they called her a baby or a freak; it was because they enjoyed it so much.

She bit the tip of her thumb and sniffled. She felt just like a double-headed goat.

## THREE
# A Goat with One Head

At lunch, she sat by herself on the grass against a tree and ate a peanut butter and jello sandwich. She preferred jello to jelly with her peanut butter.

There was a boy also sitting alone not too far away from her. She watched him try to open his bag of potato chips. He pulled and pushed the bag in every direction until she was sure that all the chips inside had been smashed to smithereens. Still, the bag would not open.

She took another bite out of her peanut butter and jello and tried to keep from laughing. Besides crying too much, Angeline also thought she laughed too much. It wasn't that she laughed a lot—just at all the wrong times. She thought watching the boy try to open his potato chip bag was the funniest thing she'd ever seen, but she didn't want to laugh at him.

He bit the bag with his teeth and jerked at it with both hands. Nothing. Still holding it in his teeth and both hands, he vigorously shook his head.

She gulped down some milk, with her eyes fixed on the boy.

Suddenly the bag burst open, and Angeline instantly burst out laughing, causing milk to squirt out of her mouth. The potato chips exploded out of the bag and onto the ground. Angeline couldn't stop laughing as she wiped the milk off her face with a napkin.

The boy stared at her. He still held part of the torn bag in one hand, part in the other hand, and part in his teeth. The potato chips were in little crumbs all around him.

Angeline did her best to stop laughing. She only managed to halt every other laugh. She hoped the boy wouldn't hit her. She didn't want to cry again.

But, to her surprise, the boy also laughed. It was a stupid, awkward laugh. He sounded like an embarrassed hyena. Then, seeing that Angeline was still watching him, he pretended to eat his empty bag of potato chips—not the potato chips, but the bag itself—as if that was all he ever wanted in the first place.

Angeline thought it was the funniest thing she'd ever seen.

Then the boy took his sandwich out of its plastic bag, threw *it* on the ground, and pretended to eat the plastic bag. Angeline couldn't stop laughing. She watched as he poured the rest of his milk onto the dirt and pretended to eat the empty milk carton. She was hysterical.

At that moment there rolled past her a tennis ball, which someone had hit all the way from the baseball field. It stopped next to the boy who was so funny.

"Hey, Goon! Get the ball!" someone called.

The boy looked at the ball.

"Get the ball, Goon!"

He didn't get it.

Philip Korbin, one of the kids in Angeline's class, walked toward the boy. He was obviously disgusted that he had to walk so far and waste the recess when he could be playing baseball.

"Come on, Goon, throw me the ball," he said.

"I'm eating," said the boy, and he pretended to eat his milk carton again.

Angeline laughed.

Philip gave her a dirty look as he walked past her and got the ball himself. "What a goon," he muttered, and started back toward the baseball field.

"Maybe if you didn't call him a goon, he would have gotten the ball for you," said Angeline.

"Shut up, Freak," said Philip. He threw the ball back toward the field and ran after it.

"I hope you strike out," said Angeline when she knew Philip couldn't hear her. She didn't know much about baseball except that the one time she got to play she struck out.

She finished her peanut butter and jello sandwich and washed it down with some milk. She still had some cookies. For the sake of his joke, the boy had thrown away his whole lunch. Angeline thought he looked hungry. "Do you feel like a cookie?" she offered. She took a sip of milk.

"I don't know," said the boy. "How does a cookie feel?"

"Pppphhhrrrwwww," laughed Angeline. This time the milk not only squirted out her mouth, it also squirted out her nose. She thought it was the funniest joke she'd ever heard.

The boy was shocked. He always told jokes, about a hundred a day, but he couldn't remember the last time anyone had ever laughed at one.

Angeline couldn't stop laughing. She didn't want lunch to ever end. "What time does your watch say?" she asked him. She hoped there was a lot of time left.

The boy put his watch next to his ear. "My watch doesn't say anything," he replied. "It can't talk."

Angeline laughed again. She thought it was the funniest joke she'd ever heard.

Again the boy was amazed. He didn't know what to think. Nobody ever laughed at his jokes. That wasn't why he told them. He didn't know why he told them, but it couldn't have been to make people laugh because nobody ever did. Sometimes someone might say, "Ha ha, very funny, Goon," but that was the closest anyone ever came to laughing. Mostly they just ignored him.

"I think you are so funny!" said Angeline when she stopped laughing.

The boy shrugged. "You're the only one," he

said. He was really glad Angeline liked his jokes. It was just too bad that he had dumped all his lunch on the ground and didn't even get the cookie that Angeline had offered. He was starving.

"What's your name?" Angeline asked.

"Goon," said the boy and then he laughed stupidly. "See, my real name is Gary Boone," he explained. "So for a joke I combined my two names and I call myself Goon." He laughed again.

Angeline didn't laugh. She didn't like being called "Freak," and was surprised to hear that he had made up the name "Goon" himself. "Do you like it when people call you 'Goon'?" she asked.

Gary shrugged his shoulders and said, "I don't know."

"Well, I'll just call you Gary," said Angeline. "I'm Angeline."

"Oh, you're the real smart kid, aren't you?" said Gary.

Angeline didn't answer.

"Angeline Persopolis," said Gary. "Hmm, I don't think I can combine those two names." But then he thought a moment and said, "Angelopolis."

Angeline laughed. She tried to think of one too. "It's too bad your name isn't Melvin," she finally said. "Then you could be the Moon."

Gary laughed. Not only did she laugh at his jokes, but she also liked to play along!

"Do you know any more good jokes?" she asked him.

No one had ever asked him that before. He tried to think of his best joke but, for the first time in his life, he couldn't think of one. His mind just went blank.

The bell rang. He quickly took off his shoe, then put it back on.

"What did you do that for?" asked Angeline.

"Do what?" asked Gary.

"Take your shoe off, then put it on again."

Gary looked around in confusion, utterly bewildered. "I don't know," he said.

## FOUR
# No Tomatoes

Angeline lay on the floor, her feet on the sofa, as she read her book about the lovelorn sailor. The sailor didn't know it, but the day after he set sail, the beautiful lady suddenly realized that she loved him too, more than anything else in the world. So she got a boat of her own and sailed the seas in search of him and was almost eaten by a shark.

Abel came home from work. "Don't hug me until I take a shower," he said, but she hugged him anyway.

"Look," said Abel. "I brought you a present. It's wrapped in plastic so it doesn't smell." He set it down on the end table at the end of the sofa.

Angeline crawled over the sofa and eagerly

tore away the plastic. It was a book called *The Philosophical Substructures of Psychological Subcultures*. With a title like that, no amount of plastic could keep it from smelling.

"Thank you," she said politely, and tried her best to look happy despite the awful odor emanating from the book.

"I hope it is smart enough for you," said Abel.

"Oh, it looks like a real smart book," Angeline assured him.

She put the book on the bookshelf along with all the other smelly books her father had given her. She wished he'd just bring her a book with a good story and lots of funny jokes.

"Gus is coming over for dinner," Abel announced after his shower.

Angeline's face lit up. "Oh, good!" Gus was Abel's partner. They drove the garbage truck together.

Abel knew she didn't like the book. Gus had told him she wouldn't like it, but he bought it anyway. Gus had told him to find a book with a good story and lots of jokes. "They don't even have to be funny jokes," Gus had said. "Angelini will laugh anyway."

When Gus arrived, Angeline let him in.

"Hello, Gus," she greeted.

"Hello, Angelini," said Gus.

"We're having chili," she told him.

"Sounds good," said Gus.

"Do you like it hot?" she asked. "I mean spicy hot, not hot hot."

"The hotter the better," said Gus.

"Me too," said Angeline, "only not too hot."

Abel was in the kitchen. He accidentally touched the hot pot of chili with his thumb. "Ow!" he exclaimed. He walked into the living room with his thumb in his mouth.

"Cute," said Gus.

"Oh, hi, Gus," said Abel. "I didn't know you were here."

"Angelini let me in. We decided we like our chili the hotter the better, only not too hot."

"You want a beer?" Abel offered.

"Thanks," said Gus.

"I want a beer, too," said Angeline.

"Don't act cute just because Gus is here," Abel told her.

She blushed. She *was* acting cute and it was because of Gus. "I'm not acting cute," she insisted. She didn't want Gus to know that she was acting cute for him.

Abel walked back into the kitchen to get the beer.

Gus poked Angeline in the side. "You can have a sip of my beer, cutie," he whispered.

She giggled.

She set the table while Gus helped Abel in the kitchen. She couldn't remember on which side to put the fork and on which side to put the spoon. It wasn't one of the things she knew before she was born.

"Do you want salad, Angelini?" Gus called from the kitchen.

"Do we have any French dressing?" she called back to him.

"No, but we have some French undressing," said Gus.

Angeline laughed hysterically.

"See?" Gus told Abel. "They don't even have to be *funny* jokes."

Abel smiled. He wished he could make Angeline laugh like Gus, but he hadn't been able to tell her a joke for a long time, either funny or unfunny. He couldn't even say "Angelini" without choking on it.

Angeline put the knives, forks, and spoons

around the table, sometimes on the left and sometimes on the right. She knew it had to be correct in one of the places. "Okay, I'll have salad with French undressing," she called. "But no tomatoes in mine."

"Sorry!" Gus called back. "There aren't any tomatoes."

"Good!" she yelled. "I *don't want* a tomato."

"Well, that's too bad," said Gus, "because there aren't any. And if you think I'm going all the way to the store just to get you a tomato—"

"But I don't want a tomato!" she screamed.

"You can scream all you want," said Gus. "You still can't have one."

"Good!" she yelled. "Excellent! I'm glad we don't have any tomatoes. I don't want a tomato. I hate tomatoes!"

Gus stood at the kitchen door and sadly shook his head. "I'm sorry to hear that, Angelini," he said. "I really am. But I'm afraid we just don't have any."

She threw her hands up in the air and gave a loud sigh. Gus laughed.

They ate the salad, chili, and soda crackers. Nobody seemed to care whether the forks, knives, or spoons were on the right side or not.

"What's the weather forecast for tomorrow?" Gus asked.

"Hold on, I'll check," said Angeline. She walked to the kitchen window and listened.

"I really wish you wouldn't do that," Abel whispered, so only Gus could hear.

"Why not?" Gus asked. "She's always right. I think it's great."

"I don't," said Abel. "Okay?"

Gus shrugged. "Okay," he said.

When Angeline got back she told them that it was going to be very hot, especially hot for October. Abel politely thanked her.

"Gus, can I ride around with you and my father in the garbage truck sometime?" she asked.

"Now, what do you want to do that for?" Gus asked. "It smells in there."

"I want to," said Angeline. "Besides, I like the smell."

"You belong in school," said Gus.

"School smells," said Angeline.

Gus laughed. "I never liked school either," he said, "but that was because I wasn't too smart. If I was as smart as you, I would have loved school. Someday you'll appreciate it."

"You never know," said Angeline.

"It's kind of tough on her now," said Abel. "All the other kids in her class are a lot older. She doesn't have any friends."

"I do too," Angeline insisted. "I have one friend. Gary Boone. He's my best friend. He's so funny. He knows so many jokes."

"Good," said Abel. "I'm glad you're finally making friends."

"Just one friend," corrected Angeline. "Just Gary. All the other kids are goons."

## FIVE
# Mr. Bone

Before, when Gary took off his shoe and put it back on and Angeline asked him why he did it and he said he didn't know, well, actually he had a very good reason. There was a pebble in his shoe. It had been there almost the whole lunch period, but because he was so amazed that Angeline had said she liked his jokes and even laughed and everything, he didn't think about the pebble. Then when the bell rang and it was time to go in, he simply took off his shoe, dumped the pebble out, and put his shoe back on. That's all. But when Angeline asked him why he did it, well, he forgot.

He was in the fifth grade, in Miss Turbone's class. He called her "Mr. Bone."

The first time he called her that, on the first day of school, it was just a joke, like Goon or Angelopolis. But like all his jokes, nobody noticed—not even Miss Turbone. After that, no matter how hard he tried to say "Miss Turbone," it always came out "Mr. Bone."

He liked her a lot. In fact, until he met Angeline, she was his favorite person at the school. Now she was his second favorite.

She had a soft face and pretty brown hair, and she wore big round glasses. He loved her glasses. He thought she looked prettier with the glasses on than without them.

"Okay, who knows the answer?" asked Miss Turbone.

"Uh-oh," thought Gary. He didn't even know the question. He looked down at his desk, hiding, like the way an ostrich hides by sticking its head in the sand. He hoped Mr. Bone wouldn't call on him.

Miss Turbone looked at Gary. She could tell by the way that he was looking down at his desk that he didn't know the answer. Some teachers, like Mrs. Hardlick, would have called on him for just that reason. Some hunters like to shoot ostriches that have their heads buried in the sand.

Miss Turbone called on somebody else.

She liked Gary. She felt sorry for him because all the other kids called him "Goon" and he didn't have any friends, but besides that, she also liked him. However, she didn't think a great deal of his jokes. She didn't know he called her "Mr. Bone." She might have thought that one was funny.

When the bell rang and all the other kids left for lunch, she told Gary she wanted to talk to him.

He walked up to her desk. "Yes, Mr. Bone."

It sounded like "Miss Turbone" to her, probably because that was what she expected to hear. "Can you stay after school today?" she asked.

"I'm not in trouble, am I?"

"No," laughed Miss Turbone. "I'm going to set up a couple of fish tanks on the back ledge. I thought you might like to help me."

"Okay," said Gary. "May I ask a friend to help us, too?"

"A friend?" questioned Miss Turbone.

"Oh, sure, Mr. Bone," said Gary. "I have lots of friends."

Miss Turbone smiled. "You may invite anyone you'd like, Gary," she said. She was glad he had made a friend.

"Her name's Angeline," said Gary. "You'll like her. She's real smart and she has a great sense of humor." He headed outside to lunch, eager to tell Angeline about setting up the fish tanks with Mr. Bone.

"Gary," called Miss Turbone.

He stopped and turned toward her. "Yes, Mr. Bone?"

"I'm your friend, too."

It was a very hot day, just as Angeline had predicted. It was the hottest October fifth since they had started recording the weather.

Abel and Gus drove up and down the city streets, one house at a time, collecting people's garbage. Sometimes Abel drove while Gus picked up the cans and dumped them in the back of the truck, and other times Gus drove and Abel did the dirty work. They traded off. Besides everything else, the hot weather made the garbage stink worse than usual, especially as the day wore on and the garbage had been out in the sun all day, baking in the heavy metal cans.

They stopped at a little park to eat their lunch. The bathrooms were locked, so they had to put their hands in front of a lawn sprinkler to wash up. It felt so good that they ran in front of the sprinkler and let it spray all over them. It was so hot that they knew that by the time they finished eating, their clothes would be dry.

Abel bit into his sandwich. "Yech!" he exclaimed. He pulled apart the bread and looked inside. "Peanut butter and jello," he muttered, realizing that he and Angeline must have accidentally traded lunches.

"What's this!" exclaimed Angeline, holding her sandwich away from her. She had taken one bite out of it. "Salami! I hate salami!"

"I'll trade with you," said Gary. "I love salami."

"Okay," said Angeline. "What do you have?"

"Salami," said Gary. "I just love salami."

They traded salami sandwiches.

"Today after school, do you want to help Mr. Bone and me set up some fish tanks?" he asked.

"Who's Mr. Bone?" asked Angeline.

"My teacher. We're setting up some fish tanks after school and Mr. Bone said you can help, too."

"Okay," said Angeline. It meant that she'd have

to take the regular city bus home instead of the school bus, but she didn't mind. She liked riding the city buses. She liked pulling the cord when it was time to signal the bus to stop. "Will they be freshwater or saltwater fish tanks?" she asked.

"Will *what* be freshwater or saltwater?" asked Gary with a slight smirk on his face.

"The fish tanks," Angeline repeated.

"The fish *what*?" asked Gary, still smirking.

"Tanks," said Angeline.

"You're welcome," said Gary.

Angeline cracked up. She thought it was the funniest joke she'd ever heard. "I hope they're saltwater," she said when she stopped laughing, "like the ocean."

"I don't know," said Gary. "Come to room twelve. You'll like Mr. Bone."

Abel and Gus finished their lunch and threw their litter in the back of the truck. They didn't have to look for a trash can. They drove one.

After school, Miss Turbone gave Gary the keys to her car and told him to bring her the package that was on the floor of the front seat. "It's a yellow car," she said. "It has a bumper sticker on the back that says SAVE THE WHALES."

As Gary walked to the parking lot, he felt special. He had Mr. Bone's keys in his hand, and he was walking to Mr. Bone's car, and was going to open Mr. Bone's car with Mr. Bone's keys. It made him feel very special. He jingled the keys while he walked.

Angeline couldn't remember if Gary had said room twelve or room twenty. She cautiously opened the door to room twelve. She thought he probably said room twelve, but then, when she opened the door and saw a lady teacher and no sign of Gary, she concluded she had gone to the wrong room.

"May I help you?" asked Miss Turbone.

"Oh. I'm looking for Mr. Bone," said Angeline.

"I'm Miss Turbone," said Miss Turbone.

Angeline's eyes widened. "You're Mr. Bone?" she questioned.

"Yes," said Miss Turbone. "You must be Angeline. Gary will be right back."

Angeline stared at her in amazement. "You're Mr. Bone?" she repeated.

"That's right," said Miss Turbone.

Angeline still couldn't figure it out. "You're Mr. Bone?" she repeated again.

"Yes," said Miss Turbone, unable to understand Angeline's confusion. "Come in. Gary is getting something for me from my car."

Angeline shrugged. "Okay . . ." she said perplexedly, ". . . Mr. Bone."

Gary returned to the classroom carrying a package. "Is this it, Mr. Bone?" he asked.

"Yes, thank you, Gary."

"Well, what do you know?" thought Angeline. "She *is* Mr. Bone."

"What's in it?" Gary asked, referring to the package he brought in. "Is it for the fish tanks?"

Miss Turbone smiled. "Why, yes, Gary," she said. "As a matter of fact, that's just what it's for."

She set the package on her desk and then they went to work setting up the fish tanks. It took them over an hour to finish both tanks, yet they still never opened the package that Gary had gotten from Miss Turbone's car.

"What are these called again, Mr. Bone?" asked Angeline.

"Fish tanks," said Miss Turbone.

"Fish *what*?" asked Angeline. She smiled at Gary.

"Tanks," said Miss Turbone.

"YOU'RE WELCOME," Gary and Angeline said together, then Angeline laughed hysterically.

They filled one tank with fresh water and one with salt water. Angeline said she liked the saltwater best and Gary said he liked the freshwater best. "Better, not best," corrected Miss Turbone. "When you compare two things, one can only be better, not best."

"Do you have any fish for them?" Gary asked.

Miss Turbone smiled. "In the box you brought from my car."

"Oh, no, Mr. Bone!" said Angeline and Gary together.

"They've been out of water all this time," said Angeline.

"They've drowned," said Gary.

Miss Turbone told Gary to open the box.

"I don't want to look," said Angeline as she peered over Gary's shoulder.

Inside the box were three big cookies, each shaped and decorated like a fish.

"One for each of us," said Miss Turbone, "for setting up the fish tanks."

"Thank you, Mr. Bone," said Angeline.

"Oh, yeah. Thank you, Mr. Bone," said Gary.

"I'll try to get real fish for the tanks tomorrow," said Miss Turbone. "Right now, I'll go get us some milk from the cafeteria for our cookies."

Angeline thought Mr. Bone was wonderful. She knew Mrs. Hardlick would never eat a fish-shaped cookie. "I don't want any milk with my cookie, Mr. Bone," she said. "I'll have a glass of salt water."

## SIX
# Secretary of Trash

The next morning, Angeline met Gary on the way to class.

"What's new?" she said.

"An animal at the zoo," said Gary.

"Huh?"

It was a joke. There is an animal at the zoo called a *gnu*, which is pronounced like *new*. So, see, when Angeline asked, "What's new?" Gary replied, "An animal at the zoo." After Gary explained it to her, Angeline thought it was the funniest joke she'd ever heard. Well, maybe not the funniest.

She hurried to class. She was looking forward to seeing Mr. Bone again, and also Mr. Bone's fish, if she got them yet, especially the saltwater ones. But first, in Mrs. Hardlick's class, they were having class elections, and she was looking forward to that too, not that she thought she had a chance to be elected for anything.

Everybody already knew that either Philip Korbin or Christy Mathewson would be elected president and that the other one would be elected vice-president. Angeline hadn't decided for whom she'd vote—probably Christy. At least she got to vote, just like all the other sixth-graders.

Besides, she didn't want to be president anyway. There was only one position that she really wanted, and that was Secretary of Trash. But then, she thought as she looked around the room, who would even nominate her, let alone vote for her?

Philip Korbin nervously approached her desk. "Hi," he said.

Angeline stared at him. She guessed he was going to ask her to vote for him, and after he had called her a freak the other day, too.

"So, uh, who you gonna vote for?" Philip asked.

"I don't know," said Angeline.

"You wanna vote for me?" Philip asked. He smiled sheepishly.

"No," said Angeline.

"I didn't mean it the other day when I told you to shut up," Philip said. "I just wanted to play baseball and Goon wouldn't get the ball."

Angeline thought a moment. "I'll make you a deal," she said. "I'll vote for you for president if you promise to nominate me for Secretary of Trash."

Philip thought it over.

"You don't even have to vote for me," said Angeline. "Just nominate me."

"Sure, what the heck," said Philip. "It's a deal."

"Okay," said Angeline.

"Angeline!" said Mrs. Hardlick. "No talking after the bell rings."

The bell rang.

"It hadn't rung yet," said Angeline.

"What did I just say about talking?" said Mrs. Hardlick, trying to cover up her mistake.

Angeline sat up and folded her hands on top of her desk. As long as they were folded, she knew she wouldn't suck her thumb. She knew she'd never be elected Secretary of Trash if she was caught sucking her thumb again. But who was she kidding? She wasn't going to be elected anyway.

As expected, Christy and Philip were each nominated for class president and they each had to give a speech. Christy was first.

"I think you should vote for me for class president because I'm very responsible, for example, I always feed and walk my dog, Toby, oh he's so cute, but for a long time we never had a dog because my parents didn't want to have to take care of him but I said I'd take care of him, but they said, no you won't, and I said yes I would too, but they said you say that now but we know you, and something always comes up, but I told them I really, truly would take care of him and then they said, okay, and so two days ago we got a dog, Toby, and he's so cute, and I always take care of him, except yesterday because I was busy writing this speech, and after all, being president is a lot more important than feeding a dog, and so I promise that if you elect me president, I won't let my dog interfere with my duties as president of the sixth grade." She took a deep breath. "Thank you."

Everyone applauded.

"Very nice, Christy," said Mrs. Hardlick. "Philip."

Philip gulped. He hadn't written a speech. He didn't know he was supposed to. He tried to think fast as he slowly walked to the front of the room. He said that he'd be a good president because "Um, I don't live too far away from school, so, um, I could rush right over in case of um, an um, emergency. I, um, live a lot closer than, um, Christy. Um, I don't have a dog." He started back to his seat. "Um, thank you."

Everyone applauded.

Philip and Christy left the room and the class voted. Angeline, as agreed, voted for Philip but he still lost. Christy Mathewson was elected president and Philip was elected, um, vice-president.

They had the elections for the other class officers; Treasurer, Secretary of the Blackboard, Secretary of Balls, Secretary of Windows, and finally Mrs. Hardlick announced, "Nominations are now open for Secretary of Trash."

Angeline's heart pounded wildly. She looked at Philip, who was looking down and away from her. "Oh," she realized. "He's not going to do it." She frowned. There was nothing she could do about it either. She had already voted for him. She couldn't take back her vote. She guessed he had probably planned it that way all along. Besides, he lost anyway. How did he know if she really voted for him? He was out of the room at the time. "Well, I wouldn't have won anyway," she thought.

Philip scratched the back of his neck and squirmed in his chair. He raised his hand. "I nominate Angeline Per . . . Per . . ." He couldn't pronounce her last name. "Purple-potamous."

Angeline beamed.

Mrs. Hardlick stared at Philip, wondering if she had heard right. "O-kay," she finally said. "Will somebody second the nomination?"

Angeline looked eagerly around the room although she already knew nobody would second her nomination. "Well, at least I got nominated," she thought.

"I second it," said Christy Mathewson.

Angeline couldn't believe it.

She gave her speech. "I think I'll make a good Secretary of Trash," she said. "My father is a great garbage collector. He works for the city. He's the best garbage collector they've got. I won't be as good as he is, but I think I can learn a lot from him." She couldn't think of anything else to say. "I hope you give me a chance. Thank you."

She won!

She was the only person nominated but she won! She was so happy, she felt like she was going to cry.

When everybody else went to recess, she had to stay inside and pick up the trash. "Make sure you pick up every last scrap of paper," Mrs. Hardlick told her.

She won! She stayed behind to pick up the trash. It didn't take very long, there were just a couple of pieces of paper and a broken eraser, but Angeline made sure she got it all.

"If only my father could see me now," she thought. "He'd be so proud.

"I won!!!!!"

## SEVEN
# The Balance of the Whole

Okay, so how did Angeline know all the things that she knew, the stuff she knew before she was born? Was she a genius? A freak? Those are each a kind of explanation. Here is another kind of explanation:

A pretty girl picks a flower. A bee returns to where the flower used to be, sees that it's gone, gets mad, and stings a man with a red beard. The man with the red beard doesn't look where he's going and bumps into a lady in curlers holding two bags of groceries. The groceries fall all over the sidewalk and the man with the red beard and several friendly neighbors all help the lady in curlers pick everything up.

Angeline might see everybody picking up the groceries and say, "Look, a pretty girl with a flower."

She was in balance with the whole.

The whole is everything and everything is part of the whole. Before everybody's born they are in balance with the whole. After they're born, most people lose their balance. Angeline didn't.

In one of the smelly books that her father gave her, there was a question that the writer of the book seemed to consider a very important question: "If a tree falls in the forest and nobody hears it, does it make a sound?" The writer said the question didn't have an answer. The truth was that the writer just didn't know the answer, but writers never like to admit that there is something they don't know. Every question has an answer, otherwise it wouldn't be a question.

Angeline knew the tree makes a sound. It is part of the whole. And everyone will eventually hear it in one way or another because everything affects everything else. You just have to know how to listen.

Angeline knew how to listen, not with just her ears but also her eyes, and nose, and mouth, and elbows, and hair, and toenails, and knees too.

She stared at Mr. Bone's saltwater fish. She hardly paid attention to the freshwater ones. Miss Turbone had gotten two kinds of saltwater fish, an angelfish and a rainbow fish. The rainbow fish was multicolored, like a rainbow. All the colors blended into one another so she couldn't tell, for instance, where the red stopped and the blue began. The angelfish was a pale pinkish blue and looked soft and feathery.

"They remind me of the ocean," Angeline said.

"Do you like the ocean?" asked Miss Turbone.

"I've never seen it," said Angeline.

"Not even on television?" asked Gary.

"We don't have a TV," said Angeline.

"What about the beach?" asked Gary. "Haven't you ever been to Mitchell Beach? It isn't far."

"No," said Angeline as she watched the fish swim about their tank.

"We go there a lot," said Gary. "How come your father has never taken you?"

"I don't know," said Angeline. "He just hasn't."

"Do you like the beach, Mr. Bone?" Gary asked.

Miss Turbone was still puzzled about how the

fish could remind Angeline of the ocean if she'd never been there. "What? Oh, yes, I love the beach."

"Me too," said Gary.

"So do I," said Angeline.

"Do you like to lie in the sun at the beach or go in the water?" Gary asked Miss Turbone.

"Both."

"Do you wear a bikini?" he asked.

Miss Turbone laughed. "Sometimes."

"Have you ever seen a whale at the beach, Mr. Bone?" Angeline asked.

"No."

"She has a bumper sticker on her car that says SAVE THE WHALES, don't you, Mr. Bone?" said Gary.

"That's neat!" said Angeline.

"No, it's not neat," said Miss Turbone. "It's terrible. The whales are all being killed off. Soon there may be none left."

"Why are they being killed?" asked Gary.

"Because people are selfish and uncaring," said Miss Turbone.

"But what do they do with them after they kill them?" Gary asked.

"Mostly they use them for dog food," said Miss Turbone, "and perfume."

"Perfume!" exclaimed Gary. "Who would want to smell like a whale?"

"I would," said Angeline. "I like the way whales smell. But that's no reason to kill them."

Miss Turbone thought about asking Angeline if she'd ever smelled a whale but thought better of it. She'd never even seen the ocean—how could she smell a whale? And yet Miss Turbone didn't doubt that Angeline knew exactly what a whale smelled like. "The perfume they make doesn't smell like whales," she said instead. "There's a very sweet-smelling substance inside the whales called amber-gris. That's what they make the perfume from."

"Oh," said Angeline. "Well, I don't want to smell like that."

"Boy, I bet you they sure get a lot of dog food out of one whale," said Gary.

"Not really," said Miss Turbone. "That's what makes it even worse."

"It's not the dogs' fault," said Angeline. "They don't know they are eating whales."

"No, it's people's fault," said Miss Turbone. "And it's not just the whales. It affects everything.

Every time a whale is killed, we're all a little worse off."

Angeline knew what she was talking about. Everyone feels it in one way or another. She was talking about the balance of the whole.

## EIGHT
# Mr. Bone Let Me Feed Her Fish

Abel and Gus finished their rounds, drove to the dump, and then waited in line behind all the other garbage trucks. It was the same thing every day. All the garbage collectors in the county finished at just about the same time so there was always a traffic jam at the dump. They heard the guy in the truck behind them blast his horn, as if he thought that would help speed things up.

"I don't know how to talk to her," said Abel.

"Angelini?" questioned Gus. "Come on, she's easy to talk to."

"For you," said Abel. "You two always hit it off great together. She likes you a lot."

"She likes you too," said Gus.

"I don't know," said Abel. "I guess so. I mean, I'm her father and I know she loves me, but that doesn't mean she *likes* me. I can't seem to talk to her. We never say more than a few words to each other."

"All you have to do is talk to her," said Gus. "There's nothing to it."

"She's been drinking salt water," said Abel. "Last night, she sat on the floor reading a book with a glass of *salt water* at her side. Why would she drink that?"

"I guess she likes the way it tastes," said Gus.

"What's there to taste?" asked Abel. "It's just salt and water."

Gus shrugged.

"I've heard that drinking salt water can make you crazy," Abel added.

"I don't think so," said Gus. "Salt doesn't make you crazy and neither does water. I don't see how salt water would."

"I don't know," said Abel. "I once read a book about some men trapped on a lifeboat and one of them drank salt water and he went crazy. It was supposed to be a true story."

"Well, I don't know," said Gus. "Ocean water

has more in it than just salt."

They moved up another space in line.

"She's too smart for me," said Abel. "I never know what to say to her."

Gus laughed. "How about asking her why she likes to drink salt water?'"

"How?" Abel asked him. "How can I ask her something like that?"

Gus laughed again. "That's a real tough problem. Maybe you could say, 'Angeline, why do you like to drink salt water?'"

"Sure," said Abel. "You make it sound so easy."

It was finally their turn. They swung the truck around, quickly dumped their garbage, then headed for the garage where they would park the truck and get into their own cars.

Angeline stood on her tiptoes and turned on the faucet over the kitchen sink. She stuck a glass under and filled it halfway with water. She picked up the salt shaker from the counter and sprinkled some salt into the glass. She took a sip, then added more salt. She took another sip and this time added more water. Another sip and she added salt again. She tasted it and smiled. Perfect. She stood back on her tiptoes and turned the water off. She brought the glass into the living room, where she slowly drank the water while she read her book.

The one-eyed pirate had captured the beautiful lady and told her that unless she married him, she would have to walk the plank. She had until sundown to decide. As the appointed hour approached, she stood at the edge of the plank with her hands tied behind her back. Her fair face stared nobly into the pink sky. "Alas," she thought, "'tis better to die with honor, than to live a life of shame."

Tears rolled out of Angeline's eyes. She wiped her nose on her sleeve. She perked up, though, as she heard her father open the door.

"Don't hug me until I take a shower," he said.

"Will you take me to the beach sometime?" she asked him.

"No," he said flatly. "No, I can't."

"What about Mitchell Beach? It's real close. Gary's family goes all the time."

"I said no," her father sternly repeated in a voice that told her she'd better not ask again.

She didn't say anything, but turned her back on him, demonstrating that she didn't think it was fair.

He walked into the bathroom and showered. He felt bad for having been so harsh with her, especially since he had decided that he would try and talk with her, just like Gus.

He put on his pajamas and robe and walked out into the living room. She was on the couch, reading. He sat down next to her. She looked up at him coldly, still mad that he wouldn't take her to the beach without even giving an explanation.

He tried to think of a way to begin. "So," he said, "what's new?"

"Oh!" she exclaimed, remembering Gary's joke. "An animal at the zoo!" She burst out laughing, and forgot all about being angry.

"Okay, fine," said Abel, even though he had no idea what she was talking about. He wanted to show her that he could talk and laugh with her, too, just like Gus. "How was school today?" he asked.

Angeline smiled as she remembered the good time she had had that day. It was one of the few days she had ever enjoyed school. "Mr. Bone let me feed her fish," she said gleefully.

"Okay, fine," said Abel. He wondered how such a simple sentence could be so confusing. He thought awhile before saying another word, then asked, "Who is Mr. Bone?"

"She's a wonderful teacher," said Angeline, happy to tell her father all about her. "She's got two fish tanks and yesterday she gave me a fish shaped like a cookie." She laughed. "I mean a cookie shaped like a fish, which I ate."

"Okay, fine," said Abel. They were talking, but it was like they were speaking two different languages. He wondered if she was trying to confuse him on purpose because he wouldn't take her to the beach. More likely, he figured, she was just too smart for him. However, he didn't want to let on, so he did his best to keep up with the conversation.

"I thought you didn't like your teacher," he said.

"I don't," said Angeline. "I hate Mrs. Hardlick. She's my teacher. Mr. Bone is Gary's teacher. She's wonderful."

He stared at her in awe. "Is Mr. Bone a woman?" he asked.

Angeline nodded. "She's real nice."

"And her name's *Mister* Bone?" Abel asked.

"Yes," Angeline told him. She knew it didn't make any sense.

"Okay, fine," said Abel. "I understand."

"You do?" questioned Angeline.

"Sure," he said. He didn't want her to know that he didn't understand, but what he didn't realize was that she didn't understand either, so that if he had just told her he didn't understand, she would have understood, but when he told her he understood, then she didn't understand.

"Explain it to me," she said.

He couldn't believe it. "What's this?" he wondered. "Now she's giving me a test!" "Explain what?"

"If she's a woman, why is her name Mr. Bone?" Angeline asked.

"I don't know!" he shouted in frustration. "You're the one who said it! Not me! She's a lady. Her name is Mr. Bone. And she teaches a school of fish. She feeds them cookies shaped like Gary."

She laughed. Angeline liked it when her father told her jokes.

Abel was too upset to notice he had made her laugh. "Okay, fine," he said again, starting all over. "What else happened in school?"

"Guess what?" she asked him.

"I give up, what?" he asked, happy to play along.

"I was elected Secretary of Trash," she said proudly.

"That sounds very interesting," he said. "Do you enjoy that?"

"Yes, it's lots of fun," said Angeline.

"Good," he said. "Do you want to tell me about it?"

"Well, see, when everyone else goes to recess, I stay inside and collect the garbage. I didn't think I'd win but Philip Korbin nominated me and Christy Mathewson seconded the nomination."

His face reddened. "You do *what*?" he demanded.

"I collect the garbage—just like you."

He felt like his insides were being ripped apart.

"I thought you might be able to give me a few pointers," she said.

"No," he told her as he stood up.

"You know," Angeline continued. "Like is it better to crumple up the paper before you throw it in the wastepaper basket?"

"No!" he repeated, much louder this time.

"No, I'm not giving you any pointers and no, you are not going to be a garbage collector!"

Angeline started to cry. "But—"

"No!" he shouted. He was furious. "That isn't what you are going to school for. Someday, Angeline, you'll be a doctor, or a lawyer, but not a garbage collector."

"You never know," she whimpered.

"Oh yes I do!" he shouted. She was afraid he was going to hit her. She'd never seen him so angry. "Tomorrow I want you to tell your teacher—Mrs. Hardlick or Mr. Bone or whatever you want to call her—that you are not going to pick up anybody's garbage except your own."

Angeline buried her face in a throw pillow. "I'll see if I can resign," she said.

"If your teacher doesn't like it, tell her to talk to me!" he told her. He looked at her crying into the sofa, then walked away into the kitchen.

She sat up. "It isn't fair!" she cried, and headed for the bathroom. "That's what you do!" She slammed the bathroom door. Then she opened it and slammed it again.

Abel turned on the kitchen sink and splashed water in his face. "I can't even talk to her," he muttered. He sighed as he thought of her crying in the bathroom. He sadly began preparing dinner.

"Do you want a milkshake with dinner?" he called. He knew she loved milkshakes. "Strawberry!"

She walked into the kitchen. Her eyes were red from crying. "No thank you," she said. "I'll have a glass of salt water, please."

"*Salt water*," he thought. He wanted to ask her why she liked to drink salt water, but he didn't know how.

## NINE
# Garbage

Christy Mathewson had her ears pierced. She came to school with little gold posts sticking through them.

"They're real gold," she said to the circle that had gathered around her. "If it wasn't real gold, my ears would turn green."

Angeline wanted to see too, but she was outside the circle. She either wanted to see Christy's gold earrings or else she wanted to see her ears turn green.

"I have to leave them in for two weeks," Christy said. "I can't take them out for anything, or else the holes will close up."

"Big deal," said Philip as he pushed his way

through the circle. "I wish your mouth would close up."

"Drop dead," said Christy.

Angeline tried to peek through the hole in the circle made by Philip but it quickly closed up, just like Christy said her ears would if she removed her earrings.

"Why don't you get your nose pierced, too?" said Philip. "That would look real good."

"Why don't you shut up," said Judy Martin.

Pretty soon the circle broke up and Christy was talking only with Judy Martin, mostly about what a creep Philip was, although they also thought he was kind of cute, but in a creepy sort of way.

Angeline walked up to them. "May I see your earrings, Christy?" she asked.

Judy Martin replied before Christy could say anything. "Get lost, Freak. Can't you see we're busy?"

Angeline flushed. She turned and quickly went to her desk. She couldn't understand why people were so mean, for no reason at all. And it wasn't even Judy whom she'd asked. It was Christy. "That's no reason to cry," she told herself, "just because she wouldn't let you see her earrings." It was just that she was always on the outside. She wished she could be an insider.

Mrs. Hardlick came in and the bell rang. Algebra was first. Algebra would have been Angeline's favorite subject except that Mrs. Hardlick killed it.

Angeline tried to think of a way to tell her that she couldn't be Secretary of Trash anymore. *I wish to resign my position as Secretary of Trash . . . Due to family obligations I must resign my position as Secretary of Trash.* She stared at a poster that she hated. She hated everything about the classroom. She thought it was the ugliest classroom in the school. And it was the ugliest school in the world. The only thing she liked about it was being Secretary of Trash. And Gary. And Mr. Bone. And Mr. Bone's fish. *I can no longer be Secretary of Trash. I regretfully resign.*

She heard Mrs. Hardlick teaching algebra, but she couldn't listen to her. She hated Mrs. Hardlick more than anything.

She thought of a joke Gary had told her. A man fell out of an airplane. Luckily, he had a parachute. Unluckily, the parachute wouldn't open.

Luckily, there was a haystack underneath him. Unluckily, there was a pitchfork in the haystack. Luckily, he missed the pitchfork. Unluckily, he missed the haystack. She laughed to herself. She thought it was the funniest joke she'd ever heard.

"Angeline!" said Mrs. Hardlick. "Do you think algebra is funny?"

"No," she replied. Actually she did think algebra was funny, but not the way Mrs. Hardlick taught it. Mrs. Hardlick killed all of the humor in it.

"It is all memorization," she heard Mrs. Hardlick say. "You have to memorize every answer for every equation."

When the bell rang for recess, she walked up to Mrs. Hardlick's desk to tell her that she had to resign. She hoped she wouldn't cry. She took a deep breath to steady herself but before she could speak, Mrs. Hardlick said, "Just where do you think you're going? You can't go anywhere until you've picked up all the garbage. I plan to give the room a very thorough inspection after recess." Then she walked out before Angeline could say what she had to say.

Angeline looked around the empty room, unsure of what to do. She didn't want to get in trouble but she didn't want to disobey her father. She started to cry.

She saw the piece of chalk, which Mrs. Hardlick had used to kill algebra, lying on the floor. She bent down, picked it up, and examined it through her tears. "Garbage," she said aloud, and dropped it into the wastepaper basket.

Mrs. Hardlick's algebra book lay open on her desk. She could tell it was the teacher's edition because it had all the answers written in it. She thought that Mrs. Hardlick probably couldn't figure out the answers herself. "Garbage," she declared, and she dropped the book in the trash.

She tore the poster off the wall. "Garbage!" she said. She crumpled it up and tossed it in the direction of the garbage pail.

Judy Martin's "A" composition was tacked on the bulletin board. She ripped it down. "Garbage!"

She ran back to Mrs. Hardlick's desk as tears fell from her face. She grabbed the blotter with both hands and threw it off the desk, knocking all of Mrs. Hardlick's books, paper, pens, pencils, paper clips, and gold stars on the floor. She broke a glass vase with a plastic rose in it. "Garbage!"

she laughed. "Garbage!" she cried.

She tore wildly through the room, pushing paper, pencils, pens, and books onto the floor. "Garbage, garbage," she repeated. She pushed all of the books off the back bookshelf. "Garbage!" She knocked over somebody's desk—she didn't know whose—then ran out of the room.

She took several deep breaths. She stopped crying but felt very light-headed. She wiped her eyes, took a long breath, and slowly exhaled.

Then, off she went to look at Mr. Bone's fish.

## TEN
# Fish

The rainbow fish gently swam about, easily and unconcerned. The angelfish glided past it. Watching them eased Angeline's mind at once. She didn't look at either Gary or Miss Turbone. She didn't think about what had just happened in Mrs. Hardlick's room, or even worse, what was going to happen. The angelfish drifted to a stop and faced Angeline head-on while it methodically breathed through its gills.

"It's watching you, too," said Gary, "just like you're watching it."

Angeline breathed with her lungs as she stared at the fish.

"I don't think it can see her," said Miss

Turbone. "I think it just sees itself reflected in the glass."

Gary and Miss Turbone watched Angeline watch the fish. They knew something was wrong. When she came in, she went right to the fish tanks without even saying hello.

"Tell her about the aquarium, Mr. Bone," said Gary.

"Yes," Miss Turbone began, "well, they have—"

Gary interrupted her. "It's this gigantic building with nothing but fish tanks, full of fish from all over the world. Some of the tanks are as big as houses with sharks and dolphins and whales."

"No whales," said Miss Turbone.

"No whales," said Gary, "but sharks and dolphins, right Mr. Bone?"

Miss Turbone nodded.

"Mr. Bone says that some people think that dolphins are smarter than people," Gary added.

"They are," said Angeline, with her eyes still fixed on the fish.

Miss Turbone laughed, not because she thought what Angeline had said was funny, but because she was startled by the matter-of-fact way she had said it.

It was one of the things Angeline knew before

she was born. Not all dolphins are smarter than all people, but some are smarter than some people—people like Mrs. Hardlick. "A duck is smarter than Mrs. Hardlick," thought Angeline.

"Tell her about the field trip," said Gary.

"Well—" began Miss Turbone.

"Mr. Bone is going to take our class on a field trip to the aquarium and she said you can come, too."

For the first time Angeline turned away from the fish tank. "Let's go," she said. "Right now! Can we? Right after recess?"

"No," said Miss Turbone, "you know that. You have to plan ahead. And of course you'll have to check with your teacher to see if you can go with us."

Angeline looked back at the fish tank. Mrs. Hardlick would never let her go. She didn't even want to think about Mrs. Hardlick. She concentrated on the fish. As she watched the rainbow fish peacefully swim around, she pretended she was in the middle of the ocean.

"Can we go to the ocean too?" she asked.

"Maybe," said Miss Turbone. "First the aquarium."

"Did you ask your father how come he's never

taken you to the beach?" Gary asked.

"He just won't," said Angeline. "I don't know why, but he won't. He won't even take me on his garbage truck."

Miss Turbone turned her head around and looked peculiarly at Angeline. She wondered what the ocean had to do with a garbage truck.

"You know why you never get hungry at the beach?" Gary asked.

"Why?" asked Angeline.

"Because of all the *sand-which-is* there!"

Angeline laughed. She thought it was the funniest joke she'd ever heard. But then her laughter suddenly stopped as she heard the bell ring.

## ELEVEN
# Mrs. Hardlick's Triumph

Angeline was scared as she walked back to Mrs. Hardlick's room. She considered going home, but she figured that that would only make matters worse. Mrs. Hardlick would call her father, and, most of all, Angeline didn't want to disappoint him. She knew that he had such high expectations of her.

She tried to think of some explanation to give to Mrs. Hardlick, but was unable to come up with one. The truth was that she didn't even know herself why she'd done what she'd done. "It's because they're killing the whales," she thought. "It affects everything."

She took a breath, then boldly opened the

door to the classroom. Immediately she burst into tears as she saw the mess she had made. She took a couple of steps, then stopped as Mrs. Hardlick coldly stared at her. It was as if Mrs. Hardlick's silent stare prevented her from going any farther.

The rest of the class were all in their seats except for Nelson Ford, whose desk Angeline had turned over. He was standing next to it, trying not to laugh. Mrs. Hardlick had evidently told everyone to leave everything exactly as it was.

Angeline wished that Mrs. Hardlick would say what she had to say and get it over with. The silence was killing her.

All the other sixth-graders tried their best to be quiet but she could hear a few muffled snickers. "The freak freaked out," someone whispered. Then someone else, thinking it was funny, copied the same joke. "The freak freaked out," she heard again.

"You did this!" shouted Mrs. Hardlick. "You can't fool me! You did it, didn't you?"

Angeline wasn't trying to fool anyone. If she hadn't done it, she wouldn't be standing there crying.

"Well, young lady, what have you got to say

for yourself?" Mrs. Hardlick demanded.

Angeline sniffled back some tears. "I wish to resign as Secretary of Trash."

Mrs. Hardlick looked furious. "Oh, you think you are so smart, don't you?" she said. "Smarter than everybody else in the class—even me!" She snorted. "Well you're not! This wasn't so smart now, was it? You don't belong in the sixth grade. A sixth-grader doesn't throw a temper tantrum when there is nobody else around. A sixth-grader doesn't rip down other people's compositions just because they got a better grade. A sixth-grader doesn't suck her thumb or cry at the drop of a hat! Babies do that! Maybe you're not as smart as you thought you were."

Angeline stood trembling and crying, waiting for Mrs. Hardlick to finish. Mrs. Hardlick had loved it when Angeline sucked her thumb and cried, but she loved this the most.

"Look at poor Nelson," Mrs. Hardlick continued. "He doesn't have a place to sit."

Nelson had to turn his face away to keep from laughing.

"I think you owe him an apology," Mrs. Hardlick demanded.

"I'm sorry," sobbed Angeline.

Nelson shrugged.

"I'm sending you home now," said Mrs. Hardlick. "I've written a note to your mother telling her what you did. I want you to bring it back tomorrow, signed by her."

"My—my mother's dead," said Angeline.

Mrs. Hardlick looked annoyed. "Do you have a father?" she asked.

Angeline nodded.

"Well then, I don't care, have *him* sign it."

Angeline shakily walked to Mrs. Hardlick's desk and took the note from her. Carefully she walked outside.

"Can I leave my desk like this, Mrs. Hardlick?" asked Nelson.

Once outside, Angeline took several steps, then collapsed against the corner of the red brick building. It felt cold against her face. She thought about her mother. She remembered her having a very soft face and great big eyes. Her mother and father went out one day while she stayed at her grandmother's. Her father came home alone. She remembered him telling her that her mother was dead. She could still see his face, pale and quivering as he told her, but he never told her how she died. She didn't want to ask.

There are some things you know before you are born, and there are some things you never know.

Christy Mathewson found Angeline just around the corner, sitting against the building. The bricks were wet from her tears. "I brought you your lunch, Angeline," she said. "You forgot it."

Angeline looked up at her and smiled. That was the second time Christy had done something nice for her, for no reason. "Thank you," she said, almost in a whisper.

"Are you all right?" Christy asked. "Maybe you should go to the bathroom and wash your face. I'll go with you if you want."

Angeline didn't have the strength to move.

"Boy, I hate Mrs. Hardlick, don't you?" said Christy. "She's so mean. That's because she's such a lousy teacher. She covers up what a crummy teacher she is by being mean."

Angeline gulped.

"You shouldn't let a crummy teacher like her upset you," said Christy. "I mean, you being so smart and everything. Someday you're going to be so brilliant and famous, anyway."

Angeline wiped her face on her sleeve. "You never know," she said.

"Philip calls her Mrs. Hardboiled," laughed Christy.

Angeline laughed.

Christy helped her stand up. They slowly walked to the girls' bathroom together.

"I like your earrings, Christy," said Angeline.

"They're real gold," said Christy. "If they weren't, my ears would turn green."

## TWELVE
# More Fish

With her lunch bag gripped tightly in her hand, Angeline waited at the bus stop in front of the school. She was still feeling a little shaky. She felt like she was losing her balance.

When the bus finally came, she stepped up onto the first step only. "Which bus do I take to the aquarium, please?" she asked the driver.

He told her, "Take this bus to Richmond Road, and then transfer to the number eight line going north. It will take you right there."

She sat down at the front of the bus. "Everything will be all right when I get to the aquarium," she thought. When the driver told her that Richmond Road was the next stop, she reached up and pulled the cord above her. That was her favorite part about riding the bus.

She got on the number eight heading north and sat by herself toward the middle of the bus. It was practically empty. She opened Mrs. Hardlick's note and read it for the first time.

*Dear Mrs. Persopolis,*

*Despite my best efforts, Angeline has been unable to adjust to the intellectual and emotional level of the sixth grade. She does not cooperate well with the other children and has stubbornly refused all special assistance I have offered her. She has been a troublemaker all year, but due to her age I have tried to be tolerant and understanding. However, today she did something which I cannot condone. While the rest of the class was out having recess, Angeline remained inside, where she proceeded to throw a temper tantrum, knocking over furniture and destroying other children's property.*

*Now, I don't know how she behaves at home, but here at school I cannot tolerate such*

*counterproductive and antisocial behavior. I*
*trust you'll see that she is properly disciplined*
*so that this kind of thing does not happen*
*again.*

*Sincerely,*
*Margaret P. Hardlick*

Her eyes burned from reading the letter. Her hand shook as she held the note in front of her, wondering what to do. But really, she didn't have any choice. She tore the note into little strips of paper and stuck them under the bus seat. If her father saw that letter, it would kill him.

"When I get to the aquarium," she thought, "somehow everything will be all right."

The bus wheezed to a stop and let off a passenger. It started up again, turned right, and passed a garbage truck going in the opposite direction.

Abel flicked on the radio and tried to find a good station.

"Donna's sister, Lisa, is in town," said Gus. "How about the four of us having dinner tonight?"

"No, I'm worried about Angeline," Abel replied.

"You worry about her too much," said Gus. "You never have any fun. You owe it to yourself."

"Yeah, well, yesterday I was worried because I never talked to her, so I talked to her like you said, and now I'm even more worried."

"Why? What did you talk about?"

Abel shook his head. "I don't know," he said. "Okay, for one thing, do you want to know what she does at school? She collects the garbage. She's school garbage collector."

Gus laughed. "She wants to be like you," he said.

"I don't want her to be like me," said Abel. "Someday she could be somebody special."

"She already is somebody special," said Gus. "And so are you. It is time you started treating yourself that way."

"All right, what do you think of this?" asked Abel. "She has an imaginary friend named Mr. Bone. *Mr.* Bone is a lady."

"Well, I'm not a psychiatrist," said Gus, "but after all, you've been both a father and mother to her for all these years. She needs a real mother."

"Oh, so now I'm supposed to marry Donna's sister," said Abel.

"All I'm saying is that you should start going out with women again, both for your sake and for Angeline. Have a good time."

"Maybe I shouldn't let her drink so much salt water," said Abel.

Angeline reached up and pulled the cord. The bus stopped in front of the aquarium. She got off and stared at the large building where, once inside, everything would be all right.

She walked up to the front door. It cost a dollar for adults and fifty cents for children. She didn't have enough. She only had enough for the bus ride home.

Sadly she leaned against a cold, black, marble statue of a seal. What was she doing there anyway? she wondered. What did she expect? It wasn't as if the aquarium would magically make everything all right.

A group of kids about her age ran toward her, laughing and screaming. They were followed by two women walking quickly after them. The women shouted at the kids to be quiet and to get into two lines. Angeline recognized it as a field trip. One of the women was a teacher and one was a kid's mother.

As the class entered the aquarium, Angeline darted to the end of one of the two lines and walked in with them. Once inside, she went off by herself.

She walked down a long hallway lined with fish tanks. The hallway was dark but the fish tanks were lighted. She saw fish of all shapes and sizes, some almost as big as she was, others smaller than her fingernails. There seemed to be every possible combination of colors. And as she walked down the corridor, somehow everything *was* all right.

There were tigerfish, dogfish, goosefish, fox-face rabbitfish, monkeyface blenny, and the beautiful but deadly turkey fish, the most poisonous fish on Earth. And as she looked at all the wondrous fishes, she was amazed by each one. Yet, at the same time, she seemed to recognize them too, as if she knew them from before she was born. She saw clown fish, convict fish, moonfish, some bumphead hogfish, and as she stopped in front of each fish tank she seemed to say, "Oh, yes, I remember you."

There were four-eyed butterfly fish, who

swam right at the very top of the water so that their eyes were half-in and half-out of water. They were able to look both above and below the water at the same time. She saw fairy basslets, who are girl fish when they're born, but are men fish by the time they die. There were Caribbean grammas, who live and swim upside down, and marbled headstanders, who do just that. She saw stonefish, who just lie on the sand at the bottom of the ocean, pretending that they are rocks, but if you step on one, you're dead.

Octopuses, sea horses, barracudas. "Yes," said Angeline very softly to herself, "I remember you." And as she looked at each fish, peacefully swimming along or lying flat on the sand, she didn't once think about Mrs. Hardlick or the note for her father or anything, and everything was somehow all right.

She passed a "Garden of Ecls." These eels were long and thin, like rubber pencils. They lived in the sand under the ocean, and only their heads, about three inches long, stuck up into the water. They looked like a meadow of tall grass, gently swaying in a breeze.

Past the fish known as the fat innkeeper, and the one appropriately called elephant lip, and the squirrel fish, toadfish, and long-snouted hawkfish, Angeline walked up a spiral staircase and emerged in the middle of a large round room. There was one, big, circular fish tank all around her. It was more like it was she who was in the tank while the fish were on the outside. There were hundreds of them swimming in a ring around her. They were all big fish and all went in the same direction, like skaters at a skating rink. Leopard sharks, giant sea bass, yellowtail, red snapper, bat rays, they all had droopy eyes and sad faces—but that was just the way they looked.

Angeline sat on the floor. She opened her paper sack that Christy had gotten for her. Christy was nice, she thought. She was glad she was president. She bit into her sandwich. This was her favorite place in the aquarium so far. It was like she was at the bottom of the ocean. She licked her lips. Lemon jello was her favorite.

A group of kids thundered up the staircase and piled into the room. It was that class on the field trip, with which Angeline had sneaked in.

"Ooh, look at this one."

"Sharks!"

"How come they all look so sad?"

They spread around the room, blocking Angeline's view in every direction. They put their faces up against the tank and knocked on the glass to try to attract the fishes' attention. But the fish paid no attention as they sadly swam in circles.

"Don't touch the glass," ordered one of the women. "You'll break it."

Angeline laughed as she imagined the glass breaking and all the fish and water pouring out. If the glass broke every time some kid pounded on it . . .

"You can't eat here," a woman told Angeline. She must have been the mother of one of the kids.

"I'm not in the class," Angeline informed her.

"Are you sure?"

Angeline nodded.

"Oh. Well, in that case," said the woman, "eat."

Angeline took another bite out of her sandwich. She watched a boy walk around in circles along with the fish. He seemed to be staying with one fish in particular, a giant sea bass. "Excuse me, excuse me, excuse me," he said as he pushed past everybody in order to stay with his fish.

A couple of the other kids saw him and

thought he had a good idea. So they picked out their own fish, too, and started walking around with them. Pretty soon everybody in the class was doing it, walking in a big circle around the room, right along with the fish. Most of the kids were laughing but some tried to frown, just like the fish.

Angeline descended the spiral staircase and continued on through the aquarium.

The Pacific hagfish slithers inside the mouths of its victims and eats them from the inside. The blind cavefish lives in caves at the lower depths of the ocean that are so dark that it doesn't know what its eyes are supposed to be used for. The African lungfish can live in mudballs, out of water. Angeline loved them all.

She saw an albino walking catfish and remembered a joke Gary had told her about a man who had a pet fish. One day the man accidentally knocked over the fishbowl and the fish fell out onto the floor. He tried to pick it up but it kept slipping through his fingers. Finally, after at least five minutes he was able to scoop up the fish with both hands and drop it back in the bowl. Luckily, it was still alive. The next day when the man came home from work he found the fish lying outside the bowl again. He quickly put it back in. This kept happening, day after day, until finally the man decided to leave the fish out for a while and see what happened. First he left it out for thirty minutes, then an hour, then two hours, then three, four, until finally he just emptied the bowl altogether and kept the fish in his desk drawer, except when he'd take it out for a walk. One day, while he was walking his fish in the park, they came to a pond. The poor fish got too close to the edge, slipped in, and drowned.

Angeline laughed. She thought it was the funniest joke Gary ever told her. She wished Gary was with her now. She thought he'd have lots of good jokes about all the different fish. She saw a chocolate catfish. She bet that Gary would have a good joke about that one.

There were glass catfish, about the size of her pinky. She could see right through them, except for their bones. And somehow, everything remained all right.

She came to a giant fish tank filled with dolphins, porpoises, sea lions, and seals, all swimming and playing together. "Yes, I remember you," she said sadly, as if before she was born, she once was a dolphin too.

Next to that one was one with an Amazon manatee in it. Back in Columbus's day, sailors used to think manatees were mermaids. These sailors had gone a long time without seeing women. A manatee looks like a shapely walrus, with hips.

A giant salamander seven feet long, little scissors-tail fish, whose tails open and close like scissors as they swim, and everything was all right at the aquarium. Puff-fish, alligator gars, zebra eels, but soon she would have to leave. Wolf fish, pipefish, a fish called snakehead and one called feather-back, school would be getting out soon. There were crabs, lobsters, anchovies, and sturgeon with their long noses and mustaches.

Sawfish with noses shaped like saws and paddlefish with noses shaped like paddles, she could have stayed there forever. There were brightly colored electric fish, so bright that their tank wasn't lit like the rest of the tanks, and flashlight fish, who emitted their own light so that they could see where they were going.

She left the aquarium. She felt fine.

Everything was still all right.

The Earth spins around at 1,037 miles per hour, she knew that before she was born, and Angeline spun around too, right along with it.

## THIRTEEN
# No Going Back

"Lay down ye weapon, sailor, or off she goes!" The sailor looked at the lovely lady with her hands tied behind her, standing at the edge of the plank. He only had to see her eyes to know that she too was in love with him. He glared defiantly at the one-eyed pirate, then slowly lowered his sword.

Angeline put her thumb in her mouth; then, catching herself, she immediately bit it. "If only I didn't suck my thumb," she thought. She examined it for teeth marks. From now on, she decided, anytime she caught herself sucking her thumb, she would bite it hard. The more it hurt, the better. "Then, maybe I'll learn."

It had been a week since Mrs. Hardlick had sent her home. She hadn't been back to school since. Instead, every day she took the number eight to the aquarium, to the bumphead hogfish, the Garden of Eels, and the circular room with all the big frowning fish. She wondered why she liked the frowning fish so much. She thought it must have been kind of like the clowns at the circus. The ones with the frowns were always funnier than those with the big smiles.

"Don't hug me until I take a shower," said Abel as he came home.

She wanted to tell him about the aquarium and about what happened in Mrs. Hardlick's class and why she couldn't ever go back there. She had been wanting to tell him about it all week, but how could she? He expected so much from her.

"Now you can hug me," said Abel as he emerged in his pajamas and robe.

Angeline hugged and kissed her father, then sneezed. The odor of his shampoo irritated her nose.

Abel always washed his hair in the shower. He had to wash all the banana peels out of his hair. Every day, all day, he felt like he had banana peels in his hair. He would look in the rearview mirror to try to assure himself that they weren't really there but he was never totally satisfied until he took his shower and washed his hair.

Angeline knew she had to tell him about school. She knew he would find out about it, anyway, someday.

"Is something wrong?" he asked her.

She stared at him for a moment, but couldn't tell him. "Oh, I hurt my thumb," she said instead.

"What happened?" he asked her.

"I bit it," she told him.

"I'm sorry. Does it hurt?"

"A little," she replied. "Not enough."

"Okay, fine," said Abel. He walked into the kitchen shaking his head. "Do you want salt water with your dinner?" he called.

"Yes, please," Angeline answered.

The phone rang. "It's for you," Abel called.

She ran into the living room and took the phone from her father. "Hello," she said.

"Hi," said the voice on the other end, "this is Goon." Gary laughed awkwardly.

"Hi, Gary."

"Hi," Gary said again. He sounded nervous.

"Where have you been the last few days?" he asked. "How come you haven't been in school?"

Angeline looked at her father cooking dinner. She couldn't talk with him there. "My socks are green," she said.

"So?" asked Gary. "You can go to school with green socks."

Angeline looked at her father again. She wished he'd leave. "My father is right here," she said. "He's not wearing any socks. He's wearing slippers."

Abel turned and looked peculiarly at Angeline.

"Oh, I get it!" said Gary. "You can't talk because your father is right there, right?"

"Yes," said Angeline.

"He doesn't know you haven't been in school?" Gary asked.

"No," said Angeline.

"Wow," said Gary, "that's really something. Well, maybe I'll see you at school tomorrow and then you can tell me."

"I doubt it," said Angeline.

"There'll be Smalayoo," said Gary.

"What's Smalayoo?" Angeline asked.

"Nothin's Smala me," laughed Gary. "What's Smala you?"

Angeline laughed. She thought it was the funniest joke she'd ever heard over a phone.

"Well, good-bye, I guess," said Gary.

"Bye."

They hung up.

Abel couldn't stand it any longer. "Why did he want to know what color socks you were wearing?" he asked.

Angeline had to think fast. "Well, see, he lost his socks, except his were blue." She quickly walked out to the living room and picked up her book.

"Did he think *I* took his socks?" Abel asked out loud, but not loud enough for Angeline to hear him.

The next day Gary walked aimlessly across the school yard, hoping that Angeline would show up. "Will you get outta the way, Goon!" someone said as he walked through their hopscotch game. "Hey! Get off the field, Goon!" as he walked across the baseball diamond. "Come on, Goon, walk around!" He went back to his classroom.

"Hello, Gary," said Miss Turbone.

"Hi, Mr. Bone," muttered Gary. "Have you seen Angeline?"

"No, I'm afraid not."

He took off his shoe, then put it back on.

"What did you do that for?" Miss Turbone asked him.

"Do what?"

"Take your shoe off, then put it back on?"

"Did I do that again?" Gary asked.

Miss Turbone smiled and put her arm around Gary. "Angeline will be back," she assured him.

"You never know," said Gary. He looked into the saltwater fish tank. He peered into it like he was gazing into a crystal ball, hoping that it would somehow tell him what happened to Angeline. But all he saw was a fish, and he didn't think that that told him anything.

"Maybe she's sick," said Miss Turbone. "Why don't you go see her after school? I bet she'd like that."

Gary knew she wasn't sick. If she was sick she could have told her father. No, she wasn't sick. It was something bigger. But he could still go over to her house after school, like Mr. Bone said.

He walked up the front stairs of the address he found in the phone book and rang the doorbell to her apartment. Nobody answered. She wasn't at school and she wasn't at home. This might be bigger than he ever even imagined. Maybe she was working for the CIA. She was certainly smart enough. That's why when he called her on the phone, she couldn't say anything in front of her father. But then, how did he know for sure that her father was even there? Angeline could have been lying about that too. All he knew for certain was that some man answered the phone—no, some person with a man's voice. Angeline wasn't a little girl at all. She was a midget Russian spy! Green socks. Green socks? It was some kind of code. She was trying to tell him something. She wanted to defect. She and agent XZ1000, who was posing as her father, were plotting to overthrow the government and . . .

"BOO!" said Angeline.

Gary stumbled down the stairs. "Have a nice trip, see you next fall," he said.

Angeline laughed.

"I never even heard you coming," said Gary. "You're as quiet as a cat."

"As a fish," said Angeline. "Do you want to come in and see where I live?" She unlocked the front door of the apartment building and they waited by the elevator.

"You have an elevator," said Gary.

"We have to," said Angeline. "We live on the fourth floor."

"We live in a house, so we don't have an elevator," said Gary.

"Do you have a backyard?" Angeline asked.

"Yes."

"Well, then, you don't need an elevator if you have a backyard. You can have a dog."

"We don't have a dog or an elevator," said Gary.

They rode the elevator up to the fourth floor. Angeline unlocked the door to her apartment and they walked inside. "Would you like some salt water?" she offered.

Gary looked around the apartment. He was thrilled to be there, just as he was thrilled the time he got to go to Mr. Bone's car. "Do you have any fresh water?" he asked.

"Yes, we have that too," said Angeline.

"I'll have fresh water," said Gary. "My father said if you drink salt water you'll go crazy. He said he read a book where a guy on a lifeboat drank salt water, then jumped in the ocean and was eaten by sharks."

"How could that be?" Angeline asked. "You don't go crazy from drinking water and you don't go crazy from eating salt, so why would you go crazy from drinking salt water?"

Gary shrugged.

"Besides," added Angeline, "fish aren't crazy and that's all they ever drink."

"I didn't know fish drank," said Gary.

Angeline went into the kitchen and made them each a glass of water, no salt in Gary's.

"Where's your room?" he asked when she returned.

"This is it," said Angeline proudly. "This is where I sleep."

"On the couch?"

"It folds out into a bed," said Angeline. "When I'm asleep it's my bedroom and when I'm awake it's the living room."

"I just have a regular bedroom," said Gary. "I wonder if my parents would let me sleep on the couch."

They sat on the floor and drank their water. Gary had a wonderful time seeing Angeline again. He was a little afraid to ask her where she'd been when she hadn't been in school. He didn't want to spoil their good time, but he finally asked her.

She told him about Mrs. Hardlick's note, and all about the aquarium, the four-eyed butterfly fish and the glass catfish, which you could see right through except for the bones.

"Aren't you ever coming back to school?" Gary asked.

"I can't," said Angeline. "I tore up Mrs. Hardlick's note and stuffed it under a bus seat. She told me I couldn't come back to class until I bring the note back, signed by my father. Since I don't have the note, I can't ever go back."

"I wish Mr. Bone would write me a note like that," said Gary. "Then I could stuff it under a bus seat and I wouldn't have to go to school."

"Mr. Bone would never write a note like that," said Angeline.

"No, I guess not."

"Besides, if I had Mr. Bone for a teacher, I'd like school."

"I guess," said Gary. "But it was a lot better when you were there too."

"I just don't fit in at school," said Angeline, "not like at the aquarium. At school, everyone calls me a freak."

"They call me a goon," said Gary.

"You call yourself that," said Angeline.

"I guess I'll always be a goon," said Gary, "but someday everybody will be sorry they ever called you a freak. You'll be somebody really great."

"You never know."

## FOURTEEN
# Mr. Bone Is on the Phone

Angeline watched the porpoises and dolphins, sea lions and seals, all playing together. She pressed her face up against the glass, squashing her nose. It would have looked funny to the dolphins, had they noticed, which they didn't. None of the fish ever noticed her.

The scissors-tail fish cleanly cut their way through the water. The sea horses galloped around the bend. The turkey fish gobbled up their fish food. And beneath the silvery moonfish, the convict fish silently escaped to the other end of the tank.

She was on the outside here too, just like at school. Even in the circular room, with all the fish swimming around her, she was on the outside. She was in the middle, but on the outside.

At school, Gary stood under a tree, near where he and Angeline first met.

It used to be, before Angeline, Gary didn't have any friends but he got along fine, telling jokes. Nobody laughed, but so what? The world spun around and he spun around too. But now he missed Angeline. Without her, his jokes, oddly enough, didn't seem funny anymore.

He kicked the tree. He had told it a joke and it didn't laugh. "What did the acorn say when it grew up? Geometry. Gee, I'm a tree." It was even a tree joke.

"It's not the tree's fault," said Miss Turbone.

Gary shrugged.

"I'm sure Angeline will be back soon," said Miss Turbone. "Did you go see her, like I suggested?"

"She's never coming back," said Gary.

"Oh?"

He sighed, then told Mr. Bone all about it. He hoped Angeline wouldn't be mad at him, but he told her everything, all about the note from Mrs.

Hardlick, and how she'd been going to the aquarium every day. "And since she destroyed the note," he concluded, "she can't ever come back." He looked sadly at Mr. Bone.

Miss Turbone didn't say a word. She just winked at him.

The garbage truck pulled into the garbage truck garage. Abel brushed the top of his head and checked in the rearview mirror one last time for banana peels. "Mr. Bone, socks, smalayoo—I tell you, Gus, it just keeps getting stranger. I'm almost afraid to go home."

"What's smalayoo?" asked Gus.

"I haven't a clue," said Abel.

They walked to their cars. "Oh, sorry," said Gus, as he purposely stepped on Abel's foot while he secretly placed a banana peel on top of his head.

Angeline made herself a glass of salt water and brought it into the living room. The one-eyed pirate brought his prisoners to a secret cove, where he tried to think of the best way to kill them. He and his crew laughed and sang ribald songs as they drank rum and brandy. The sailor didn't let on that he had managed to untie the rope around his hands.

Abel came home. "Don't hug me until I take a shower," he said.

Angeline laughed when she saw him. "Make sure you wash the banana peel out of your hair," she said.

Abel was amazed—more amazed than when she played the piano or beat a computer at chess. She knew about the banana peels! How did she? How could she? It made him feel extraordinarily close to her. He hadn't felt that way for a long time.

But then he felt the top of his head. There really was one! He threw it away, in the trash in the kitchen, underneath the sink. The phone rang. Angeline watched as he answered it. "Hello," he said.

"Hello, Mr. Persopolis?" It was a woman's voice.

"Yes."

"I'm Miss Turbone. I'm a teacher at Angeline's school."

He dropped the phone and stared at Angeline.

"She says she's Mr. Bone," he whispered. It was as if everything imaginary were suddenly turning real—first the banana peel, now Mr. Bone. He retrieved the phone.

"Uh-oh," mouthed Angeline.

"Hello, are you there? Hello?" said Miss Turbone.

"Hello," said Abel. "Sorry, we were temporarily cut off. So, what can I do for you . . ." He paused. ". . . Mr. Bone?"

"I would like to talk to you about Angeline," she said.

Abel looked around the room in disbelief. "I would like to talk to you, too, Mr. Bone."

"Good," said Miss Turbone. "I think it would be better if we talked in person. Perhaps I could come over there later this evening?"

"Okay, fine." He gave her directions.

"Good. I'll see you in, say, two hours?"

"Okay, fine."

"Good-bye."

"Good-bye, Mr. Bone."

He hung up the phone and began talking to himself. "That's it, Abel," he said. "It's all over. You've finally cracked."

He took his shower and washed the rest of the banana peels out of his hair. "It's no wonder I have banana peels in my hair," he said loudly. "My head is full of bananas."

Angeline watched him shave. "Is Mr. Bone coming over here?" she asked him.

"So she said," said Abel.

She liked to watch her father shave. It fascinated her, the way he scraped the creamy white lather off his face while the hot water steamed up the bathroom. "Are you shaving because of Mr. Bone?" she asked.

"Sure, why not?" Abel replied. He slapped some after-shave lotion on his face, and also on Angeline's.

She shrieked with delight. "Ooh, it tingles."

He put on a clean shirt, and tie too, for Mr. Bone.

"You look so handsome," said Angeline.

They were both beginning to feel very excited. Abel took a couple of deep breaths to try to calm himself. "Okay, one last time," he said. "Who is Mr. Bone?"

"She's a teacher," Angeline replied. "She teaches Gary's class."

"Okay, fine."

Angeline didn't know why she was so excited that Mr. Bone was coming over, except that she hadn't seen her for a long time. It only meant that she would get into trouble and would have to go back to Mrs. Hardlick's class. Still, the thought of Mr. Bone coming here, to her apartment, thrilled her.

Abel didn't know why he was so excited either. Maybe it was because Angeline was so excited, or maybe it was because he'd find out who this mysterious person really was. "Or maybe," he thought, "maybe it's because I'm just plain loony."

They both forgot all about eating dinner.

When the bell rang, Angeline hit the button to let Mr. Bone into the apartment building. Then she waited by the door for Mr. Bone to come out of the elevator. "Over here, Mr. Bone!" she called.

"Come on in," she invited. Even though she knew it meant she'd get into trouble, she remained absolutely delighted to see her, just the same.

"This is my father."

Abel and Miss Turbone shook hands.

"Mr. Persopolis," said Miss Turbone.

"Mr. Bone," said Abel.

There are some people who are so cold and unfeeling, like reflections in a mirror, that they might as well be imaginary. But as Abel shook Miss Turbone's hand, he could feel her warmth. And he could see it in her face. And as they talked, he could hear it in her voice.

"Call me Melissa," she said.

Abel was glad her name wasn't Howard or Robert or Frank. He thought Melissa Bone was a nice name. He told her to call him Abel.

"Call me Angeline," laughed Angeline.

Melissa sat on the sofa.

"That's my bed," said Angeline. "It folds out."

Melissa smiled. "It's very comfortable."

"So now, what can we do for you Mr.— Melissa?" Abel asked. His tie was strangling him. He didn't know why he had put it on in the first place.

"Maybe it would be better if we could talk alone," she suggested.

Angeline was sent to her father's bedroom. She took her book with her although she had no intention of reading it. She sat with her ear next to the door and listened.

"I don't know where to begin," said Melissa. "Has Angeline told you where she's been for the past week?"

"Where she's been?" Abel repeated.

"She hasn't been in school."

"No," said Abel as he turned and looked toward his bedroom door. "No, I didn't know that."

"She's been going to the aquarium," Melissa informed him.

Angeline knew, of course, that Mr. Bone would know that she hadn't been in school. What she couldn't figure out was how Mr. Bone knew she'd been going to the aquarium. It amazed her.

"I only know what Angeline's teacher, Mrs. Hardlick, told me about it," said Melissa, "and to be perfectly honest I don't believe half the things that Margaret Hardlick says." She then related to Abel Angeline's final act as Secretary of Trash and the subsequent note that Angeline was supposed to have signed by her mother.

"Her mother's been dead for over five years," said Abel. His tie was driving him crazy. He stretched his neck in all directions. "Excuse me," he said, "would you mind if I took off my tie?"

"Oh yes, terribly," she answered.

"Oh, all right then," said Abel. He kept it on.

Melissa laughed. "I'm kidding," she told him.

Abel smiled foolishly. He took off his tie and hurled it across the room. He unbuttoned the top button on his shirt and let out an exaggerated sigh of relief. "Much better," he said.

"I could never figure out why men wear those things in the first place," said Melissa. "And they say that women are such slaves of fashion."

Maybe that was why she called herself "Mr. Bone," thought Abel. It was some kind of women's liberation. He returned to the topic of conversation. "I never saw the note," he said.

"I know," said Melissa. "Angeline stuffed it under a bus seat."

Incredible! thought Angeline from behind the door. Mr. Bone knows everything!

"I told Mrs. Hardlick that I would speak to her mother—to you—in lieu of the note," said Melissa.

"Well, thank you," said Abel. "I'll see that Angeline is punished."

Melissa and Angeline each winced at that. "Please don't get me wrong, Abel," said Melissa, "she's your daughter. But I didn't come all the way over here so that Angeline would be punished."

On the other side of the door, Angeline wiped her forehead. "Way to go, Mr. Bone," she whispered.

"I'm all ears," said Abel.

Melissa smiled at that expression. "I guess I just wanted you to be aware of the situation," she said.

"Well, I'm aware of the situation," said Abel. "Angeline gets herself into lots of situations. And I blow every one of them."

"Judging by Angeline," said Melissa, "you must be doing something right."

"Really?" said Abel. "You think so? Even though she's been going to the aquarium?"

Melissa laughed. "If I had Margaret Hardlick for a teacher, I'd go to the aquarium, too."

Abel smiled. "Really? Okay, so now what do I do?"

"What do you think about switching Angeline to my class?"

Behind the door, Angeline vigorously nodded her head.

"That's the fifth grade, isn't it?" asked Abel.

Melissa said it was.

"I don't know," said Abel. "No offense, but I hate to see her move backward. She has so much potential; that's what really scares me. I don't want to do anything to blow it. I hate to send her back a grade just because you're such a pretty, er—" He stumbled over his words. "A pretty nice person, er, I mean teacher." He smiled.

"Thank you, Abel. I think you're nice also." Angeline beamed.

Abel took a deep breath. "Okay, fine," he said. "What happens next year?" he asked. "She'll be in the sixth grade all over again, won't she, with Mrs. Hardlick?"

"Who knows where she'll be next year?" said Melissa. "Right now, she's smart enough to be in college, yet emotionally, she needs to be with kids her own age. That's the whole problem. She doesn't fit anywhere."

Angeline agreed with that. She was always on the outside, even now, behind the door.

"So why the fifth grade?" Abel asked.

"Because," Melissa said, shrugging modestly, "because, like you said"—she smiled—"I'm a nice teacher."

"Yes, I bet you are," said Abel.

They decided to leave it up to Angeline. She bolted out from behind the door. "I want to be in Mr. Bone's class," she announced.

"Okay, fine," said Abel.

Miss Turbone told Angeline that she might have to wait a couple of days before all of the administrative stuff could be completed. In the meantime, she would have to return to Mrs. Hardlick's class.

"Okay, fine," said Angeline.

It didn't occur to any of them, at the time, that Angeline might have been better off waiting at home or at the aquarium or anyplace else except Mrs. Hardlick's class, until the administrative stuff could be completed.

They didn't think that one or two days would matter.

## FIFTEEN
# Otherwise Known as Mr. Bone

Abel offered to walk Melissa out to her car. She said it wasn't necessary but he insisted. "I don't know how safe the streets are this time of night," he said.

They didn't speak, or even look at each other, as they rode down in the elevator. Elevators do that to people. But once outside in the cool night air, Abel finally asked the question he had wanted to ask all night.

"Melissa, why do you call yourself Mr. Bone?"

She wasn't sure she understood his question. "At school," she replied, "the students are not supposed to call their teachers by their first names, although I really wouldn't mind if they wanted to call me Melissa."

He wasn't sure he understood her answer. "No. Why *Mister?*" he asked.

"What?"

"Why Mr. Bone? Why not Miss Bone?"

"Miss Bone?" she questioned. "Mr. Bone?" She looked at him with utter astonishment. "Mr. Bone," she repeated. "Mr. Bone!" she exclaimed. She laughed so hard she had to grab his arm to steady herself.

Abel didn't know what to think.

"Does Angeline call me Mr. Bone?" she asked. She couldn't believe it.

"Yes," said Abel. He felt embarrassed but didn't know why.

"And you call me Mr. Bone, too?" she asked.

He shrugged. "I guess. You answered to it."

She laughed again and buried her face in his shoulder.

He wished he knew what was so funny.

Just for a moment she felt like kissing him. Instead, she squeezed his arm. "Abel," she said, "my name is Melissa Turbone, otherwise known as Miss . . ." She paused for emphasis. "Turbone." Her mouth dropped open. Just then, when she had said her name, even *with* the pause for emphasis, it did sound to her like she said "Mr. Bone." "You know, you're right!" she remarked. "No matter how you try to say it, it still comes out Mr. Bone!"

"See?" said Abel.

"I never noticed that before. Now I'll never be able to say Miss Turbone again. Ahhh!" she screamed and quickly covered her mouth with her hand. "What I just said, Abel. It sounded like Mr. Bone, didn't it?"

He smiled and nodded.

"Oh my," said Melissa.

They reached her yellow car with the bumper sticker on the back that said SAVE THE WHALES. She got in. "Well, it was very nice meeting you, Abel."

"Nice meeting you," Abel smiled, "Mr. Bone."

She winked at him, then drove off.

He walked back to his apartment, whistling. "Melissa Turbone," he thought. "That's a nice name, too."

When he got upstairs, both he and Angeline suddenly realized that they were starving!

## SIXTEEN
# Crazy Driver

It was a clear crisp fall morning, splashed in sunshine, and although most of the birds had already headed south for the winter, there were still a few to be seen, chirping above the garbage truck. The fallen leaves crackled under its wheels as it rolled down the road, lined on both sides by trees, red and gold and brown, and by garbage cans, silver and bright, billowing with garbage.

The truck stopped and both Abel and Gus got out and walked to the nearest garbage. Abel, smiling as he had been all morning, like the cat that ate the canary, breathed in the fresh scent of fallen leaves mixed with old coffee grounds and crusty eggshells. "Well, I met Mr. Bone last night," he said.

"And?" questioned Gus.

"She's beautiful," said Abel, grinning foolishly. He lifted a metal can and dumped it in the back of the truck. "Light as a feather," he commented.

Gus smiled at his partner. "Oh yeah?" he said.

Angeline awoke on her sofa bed and instantly sat up, as if from a terrible dream. "Why do I have to go back to Mrs. Hardlick's class at all?" she asked aloud, although she knew her father was already at work. "Why can't I just wait a couple of days, until everything is straightened out, and then go straight to Mr. Bone's class?" She frowned. "I mean Miss Turbone's class," she muttered.

Last night, her father had told her Mr. Bone's real name. He had come in whistling, and humming the parts he couldn't whistle; she had never seen him so happy. It made her smile and laugh just to look at him. But when he told her Mr. Bone's true name, the smile dropped from her face.

"Miss . . . Turbone," Abel had explained.

"Oh," said Angeline. "That's too bad."

It was like he had told her there was no Santa Claus.

She got out of bed and tried to get ready for

school as quickly as she could, but it seemed to take her forever. She knew that everyone would look at her funny and stare at her when she returned to class after all that had happened. She didn't want to call extra attention to herself by walking in late. Yet she couldn't get herself to move quickly. She nearly missed her school bus.

When the bus stopped in front of the school, she was the last one to get out of her seat. Very slowly she walked down the aisle between the rows of seats, and then stepped down the stairs to the parking lot. She put both feet on one step before moving down to the next one.

She continued to walk slowly across the parking lot and into the school yard. "You better walk faster," she told her feet, "so I'm not late."

She walked so slowly she was almost walking backward. On all sides, kids hurried past her to their classrooms, until, at last, she was the only one still outside. Then the bell rang.

"See?" she said. "Now I'm late."

She stood outside Mrs. Hardlick's door. She stood outside Mrs. Hardlick's door. She stood outside Mrs. Hardlick's door.

She opened it.

". . . the capital of—" Mrs. Hardlick broke off

in the middle of her sentence when she saw Angeline. She watched her walk to her seat in the back of the room. Everyone stared at her, just as she knew they would. "You're late," said Mrs. Hardlick.

She didn't say anything. She saw Christy Mathewson give her a tiny wave, and that made her feel a little better.

"All right," said Mrs. Hardlick, "let's see if we can get through the rest of the day without your disrupting my class again, shall we?" Mrs. Hardlick looked down at her book. "Where was I? Okay. Who can tell me the capital of France?"

Nobody raised a hand. Angeline knew the answer but she didn't dare raise her hand.

"Oh, come on class," urged Mrs. Hardlick. "What's the capital of Paris—er, I mean what's the capital of France?"

Still nobody raised a hand.

"Geez!" thought Angeline. "She even told them the answer!"

Philip finally raised his hand. "Chicago?" he tried.

"No, I'm sorry," said Mrs. Hardlick, "but that was a good guess. Chicago is the capital of Illinois."

Springfield was the capital of Illinois, but Angeline knew better than to tell that to Mrs. Hardlick.

Judy Martin raised her hand. "Cleveland?" she tried. "Or Massachusetts?"

"No, but those were both very excellent choices, Judy," said Mrs. Hardlick. "It shows you're thinking. Cleveland is the capital of Ohio and Massachusetts is a state."

Columbus was the capital of Ohio.

Finally Mrs. Hardlick proudly told the class that the capital of France was Paris. "Write that down in your notebooks so you don't forget."

Angeline realized something she knew all along. Mrs. Hardlick liked it when the class gave wrong answers. Mrs. Hardlick liked to be able to give the right answer herself.

"What's the capital of Lon—I mean, what's the capital of England?" asked Mrs. Hardlick.

"I don't believe it," thought Angeline. "She almost gave it away again."

Angeline raised her hand, hoping that Mrs. Hardlick would call on her so she could give a wrong answer, but Philip also had his hand raised. "London," he said.

"Yes, that's right," said Mrs. Hardlick, sounding a little disappointed. She should have called on Angeline. Angeline would have said Mexico City.

After that, Angeline raised her hand to every question but Mrs. Hardlick refused to call on her, until she had no other choice.

"Who was the second president of the United States?" she asked.

Angeline's arm shot up like a rocket.

Mrs. Hardlick looked around. There was nobody else to call on. "Okay, Angeline," she said dejectedly.

"Betsy Ross!" said Angeline.

Mrs. Hardlick smiled. "No, I'm sorry," she said, "but that was good thinking! That is a correct answer, but to a different question. The second president of the United States was—now write this down in your notebooks—John Quincy Adams."

Angeline wrote it down even though she knew that John Quincy Adams was the sixth president and that just plain John Adams was the second. But she had to wonder how Mrs. Hardlick could get it wrong when she had the answer written right there in front of her.

Mrs. Hardlick called on Angeline several more times.

"What was Mark Twain's real name?"

"Clark Kent."

"How much is twelve times twelve?"

"Twelve."

"No, I can see how you reached that answer but I'm afraid it is incorrect. It shows you were thinking."

"Thank you, Mrs. Hardlick," said Angeline. She was glad that she'd be out of this classroom and away from Mrs. Hardlick in a couple of days. Even though she had discovered how to get along, it was beginning to drive her crazy.

The birds sang, the leaves crackled, and the garbage truck came screeching around a corner, nearly hitting a parked car.

"Hey, slow down," urged Gus as he held on to the dashboard.

Abel turned and looked at him absentmindedly. "Sorry," he said.

"Will you watch the road!" Gus shouted back at him. He buckled his seat belt. It was something he rarely did, since he had to keep getting in and out of the truck to collect the garbage.

"Sorry," Abel said. "I wasn't paying attention. I was thinking about—"

"Stop!" yelled Gus.

Abel slammed on the brakes. The truck screeched to a sudden halt, causing garbage to fly out over the top of it and onto the street.

Gus shook his head and sighed. "You just missed that dog," he said. "Did you even see it?"

"Sorry," said Abel. "I guess I was thinking about Melissa."

"No kidding," said Gus. He unfastened his seat belt, and he and Abel got out of the truck to pick up the garbage that had fallen out. Most of it had fallen out of the garbage bags, so they had to pick up each bit of garbage off the street.

Abel picked up a milk carton and an empty can of peas. "Beautiful day, don't you think?" he asked.

"Lovely," muttered Gus as he tried to pick up a broken jar of tomato sauce without cutting himself. Actually, he was glad to see that Abel had a woman on his mind.

"Did I tell you about Melissa?" Abel asked.

Gus laughed. "You haven't stopped talking about her."

"Well, I just think she'll make a good teacher for Angeline, that's all."

"Oh, I see!" said Gus. "You're just worried about Angeline having a good teacher!"

"That's right!" Abel insisted. "Why? What else did you think?"

Gus smirked. "Oh, nothing."

"What? Did you think I was in love with her or something?"

"Why would I think that?" asked Gus. "You're only looking for a good teacher for Angeline."

"That's right," said Abel.

"One that's beautiful," Gus added.

"Yes," said Abel. "No. Oh, you don't understand."

Gus laughed. They picked up the remainder of the garbage off of the street, then started to get back into the truck.

"Other side," said Gus. "I'll drive."


Gary Boone stared sadly at his shoes. It was recess again, and he had nothing to do. He didn't even like looking at Mr. Bone's fish anymore.

They reminded him of Angeline. Everything reminded him of her. He wondered if he'd ever see her again. He hadn't told even one joke all day.

Suddenly two hands covered his eyes. "Guess who?" said a familiar voice from behind.

He didn't have to guess. He knew who it was, although he couldn't believe it. He felt so happy he almost burst into tears. He couldn't speak for a moment, then said, "Jim Nasium."

Angeline laughed. It was the funniest joke she'd ever heard.

Gary turned around in delight. "You're back!" he declared.

"So are you!" said Angeline.

"I've always been here," said Gary.

"You're back to me," said Angeline.

Gary was flabbergasted. "When, what—" He didn't know what to say first. "What did Mrs. Hardlick say? Is she being mean to you?"

"I figured it out," said Angeline. "All I have to do is answer every question wrong, and everybody likes me."

"Gee," said Gary. "I do that all the time and nobody likes me."

"I like you," said Angeline.

Gary smiled at her. His eyes were misty. He liked her, too.

"Do you have any new jokes?" she asked him.

He cried.

## SEVENTEEN
# Different Directions

As Angeline walked back to class, Judy Martin was standing in the doorway. "What's the matter, Freak?" Judy teased. "You missed a couple of problems."

"I don't know," Angeline mumbled.

"How did it feel?" Judy continued. "Was that the first time you ever missed one? What was it like?"

"I don't know," Angeline said again.

"You don't know!" declared Judy. "I guess you're just not so smart anymore, are you?"

Philip Korbin butted in. "Yeah, Judy," he said. "She's almost as dumb as you."

"Shut up."

Christy Mathewson once again came to her rescue. "She's missed a week of school," she said. "It will just take her awhile to catch up." She walked with Angeline to her seat.

"You knew the correct answers, didn't you?" Christy asked her when they were alone.

"I don't know," said Angeline.

"You shouldn't give the wrong answers when you know they're wrong," said Christy. "That's just like lying."

"No talking!" declared Mrs. Hardlick. "The bell has rung."

Christy quickly and quietly took her seat.

Mrs. Hardlick told them to get out their history books. It wasn't like Christy had said, thought Angeline. She wasn't lying. She only gave the wrong answers because that way Mrs. Hardlick wouldn't hate her. It had seemed like such a good idea. Now, Christy made her feel bad about it.

"Who invented the cotton gin?" asked Mrs. Hardlick.

Angeline glanced over at Christy, then looked straight at Mrs. Hardlick. She raised her hand.

"Yes, Angeline?" said Mrs. Hardlick.

Angeline thought a moment. "Jim Nasium," she said.

The world spun around at over a thousand miles an hour and Angeline felt like she was spinning around too—in the opposite direction.

"So when are you going to ask her out on a date?" Gus asked.

Abel felt his heart leap into his mouth. "Who?" he asked.

"You know who," said Gus. "Mr. Bone."

Abel laughed. Actually, he giggled. "Oh, no," he said. "I can't, she won't, she's—no, I can't do that." He stared out the window over the door.

"Okay, fine," said Gus.

"You think, maybe?" asked Abel. "Could I? No. She's Angeline's teacher. I can't go on a date with Angeline's teacher, can I? Can I?"

"She's not her teacher yet," said Gus. "You can ask her out for tonight. Call her now."

"NOW!" shouted Abel. "I can't ask her out now." He looked at Gus as if he were crazy. "I smell like garbage!"

"That's the wonderful thing about telephones," said Gus. "She can't smell you."

"No, you still can't go out with your kid's

teacher. It's probably against the law. Besides, she probably already has lots of dates for tonight or is busy grading papers."

"Lots of dates for tonight?" questioned Gus.

"Okay, then, what about Angeline? What would she think if I went out with her teacher?"

"She likes Mr. Bone," said Gus.

"That's just it," said Abel. "And I told you, her name's not Mr. Bone. It's Melissa Turbone."

"That's too bad," said Gus.

"It's just that she'll finally have a teacher she likes, and I don't want to do anything to blow it for her. It might be very traumatic for her and result in deep psychological implications."

Gus stopped the truck.

"What are you doing?" asked Abel. "What are we stopping for?"

Gus pointed at the row of industrial trash bins. "Garbage, Abel, remember?"

Angeline ate lunch with Gary, Miss Turbone, and Miss Turbone's fish. She hardly said a word as she ate. She thought about what Christy had said, and about Mrs. Hardlick, and none of it seemed to make any sense.

"So how does it feel to be back in school?"

Miss Turbone asked her.

She didn't answer her. She stared at the fish. She felt like she needed to go back to the aquarium or, better still, to the ocean. She sipped a glass of salt water.

"We'll be taking that field trip to the aquarium in three weeks," said Miss Turbone.

"I don't know," said Gary. "That aquarium sounds fishy to me."

Angeline didn't laugh. She didn't think it was a very funny joke.

Someone knocked on the door and Gary opened it. "Hey, Goon," said a kid from his class, all out of breath. "Is Miss Turbone in here? Miss Turbone, there's a phone call for you in the office."

Miss Turbone laughed but nobody knew why. It was because when the boy said "Miss Turbone," it sounded to her like "Mr. Bone."

The office was nearly empty when she got there. Everyone except one secretary was at lunch. Miss Turbone walked into the vice-principal's office and picked up the phone. "This is Mr. Bone."

"Melissa?"

"Yes," she said, unable to place the voice.

"Hi, this is Abel Persopolis, Angeline's father."

"Oh, hello, Abel," she answered warmly. "I was just having lunch with Angeline."

Abel nodded.

"You haven't changed your mind about switching her to my class, have you?" she asked him.

"No," said Abel. He was calling from a pay phone at a gas station. Gus had parked the truck across the street and told him he wouldn't move until Abel called up Mr. Bone. "So, you got home all right last night?" Abel asked. He was sweating.

"Yes. Why? Is it a dangerous trip?"

"Oh, I don't know," said Abel. "You never know."

"I had no problems," she assured him.

"Well, I just thought I'd call and make sure," he said.

"Thank you, Abel. That is very sweet."

"Okay, fine," he said, thinking that he could now say good-bye to her and then tell Gus that she didn't want to go out with him because of the psychological problems it would cause for Angeline.

"Is that all?" Melissa asked him.

He paused. "Yes. No." He took a breath. "Would you like to have dinner with me tonight?"

"Tonight?"

"Yes. See, I wanted to go out with you before Angeline switched to your class. I hear it might be against the law to have dinner with your kid's teacher."

Melissa laughed. "I'd love to have dinner with you tonight," she said. "We'll have to keep our eyes out for the cops, just the same," she added, playing along with his joke.

Since she knew the way to his apartment, she said that she'd drive. "It's too hard to give directions to my condominium."

Abel walked back to the truck.

"Well?" Gus asked eagerly.

"What?" Abel asked innocently.

"C'mon," Gus demanded. "Wha'd she say?"

"Who?" asked Abel.

"Just tell me what happened and stop being so funny!"

"I'm not being funny," said Abel.

"I know," said Gus. "You're not the least bit funny. So will you tell me what she said?"

Abel shrugged. "We're going out tonight," he said very casually.

The bell rang, signifying that lunch was over. Miss Turbone looked around the vice-principal's office. "I hope it's not against the law," she said aloud, then quickly walked back to class.

Out on a sidewalk a mailman turned and watched a garbage truck drive down the street and he wondered why it kept on honking its horn.

Mrs. Hardlick told her class that she had some bad news. "I just found out," she said, "that Angeline will soon be leaving us."

"Ohhh," said the class, as if they were truly sorry to see her go.

"Is she moving?" someone asked.

"Where are you going, Angeline?" asked Judy Martin.

"She'll still be at school," said Mrs. Hardlick. "She's going into Miss Turbone's fifth-grade class."

"That's not fair," said Philip Korbin. "She's smart enough to be in the sixth grade, easily."

"She sure is," said Nelson Ford.

"I know," said Mrs. Hardlick, "and just when she was beginning to show some real progress. Isn't that always the way? What's the matter, don't you like it here, Angeline?"

Angeline stared at her, wide-eyed.

"Do you think the fifth grade is better than the sixth grade?" Mrs. Hardlick asked. "Well, it's not. The sixth grade is best. The second grade is better than the first grade. And the third grade is better than the second grade. And the fourth grade is better than the third grade. And the fifth grade is better than the fourth grade. And the sixth grade is best!"

Angeline was dumbfounded. What was this nonsense?

"You're too smart for the fifth grade," said Mrs. Hardlick. "You belong here with me."

Angeline stared at her in disbelief. She felt as if the walls were closing in on her.

"If you want," said Mrs. Hardlick, "I'll talk to the principal about it. I'll ask him to let you stay here."

"No," Angeline whispered.

"Pardon?"

"No!" she shouted. She didn't mean to shout

so loud. She started to cry. "Excuse me," she said. She stood up. "Excuse me. Excuse me. Excuse me." she ran out of the room.

She ran across the school yard to the bus stop. Her heart was thumping and she was breathing very fast. Her head spun. She paced quickly in front of the bus stop. Fortunately she didn't have to wait long.

She got on a bus, walked to the back, then walked back to the front and sat down somewhere near the middle. She never pulled the cord. She rode the bus all the way, as far as it went, past the high school, past the shopping mall, past the train station, past the tire store, past the hospital, all the way to the ocean.

## EIGHTEEN
# Where's Cool Breezer?

When the bus reached the ocean, Angeline was the only passenger left. It stopped across the street from Mitchell Beach, in front of a liquor store.

She hopped off the bus and gazed across the street. She still couldn't see the ocean but she could see the sand. And she could smell the ocean. Its smell surrounded her. It was just as she had remembered.

She stepped blindly into the street. A car slammed on its horn, screeched, and swerved around her. She was lucky she wasn't run over.

She ran across the street and to the top of a sand dune at the entrance to Mitchell Beach.

From there, at last, she saw it, green and blue and brown, rolling and crashing against the shore. The water stretched out for as far as she could see, until it met the sky. She felt the ocean breeze blow through her hair. She smiled.

Despite the Indian summer weather, the beach was empty except for a lone fisherman who was fishing off Mitchell Pier. She wondered who Mitchell was, that he had a beach and a pier named after him. She wondered if that's who the fisherman was.

She yelled as loud as she could and ran full speed down the face of the sand dune, then continued out across the sand until she fell over. She laughed as she sat up, spitting sand out of her mouth. She took off her shoes and socks and left them there at the place where she had fallen.

She walked very slowly to the ocean. She walked slowly, not because she was afraid, but just the opposite: she wanted to savor each step. She stopped just outside the reach of the white water and rolled her pant legs up to her knees. Her skin tingled.

A wave broke toward her and she quickly backed away from it. She returned as the water receded and stepped in up to her ankles. "Yikes!" she exclaimed as she jumped out of the water. Then she walked back in. It didn't feel as cold the second time.

She continued in up to her knees, just below her rolled-up pants. She bent over and stuck her arms in too. Then she splashed her face with the salt water. As she did that her pant legs unrolled into the water. She laughed and leaned farther over so her hair could get wet, too.

A wave came crashing toward her. She ran away from it as best she could. She escaped the worst, but she got splashed by the white water. She laughed. She jumped down on the sand, rolled over, and sat up facing the ocean. Her clothes were all wet and salty and sandy. Wherever she looked, the ocean went on and on and on and on forever. She wondered where she had left her shoes and socks.

She got up and walked down the beach toward the pier. Her pants felt coarse as they rubbed against her legs. She could taste the ocean water in her mouth.

She had to crawl up a steep sand dune and step over some rocks in order to get onto the pier. She could have gotten to it more easily from the street, but she didn't want to leave the beach. She had finally found a place where she felt she belonged, and she didn't want to leave it.

She climbed up onto the pier, slipped under the wood railing, and walked out toward the end. She took a deep breath of ocean air. She wished she hadn't lost her sneakers. She had to walk carefully on the pier. She didn't want to get a splinter in her foot. She also had to beware of the rotting remains of dead fish. She didn't want to step on a fish head, barefoot.

She watched the fisherman as he tried to reel in a fish. She thought it must have been a big one, the way his line was all bent over. She stood right next to him to get a better view.

He glanced quickly at her. "Howdy," he said. His voice was high and raspy. A line of sweat dripped down his dirty forehead, under a soggy wool cap. He smelled like stale alcohol. There was half a bottle of whiskey and lots of beer cans, some full, some empty, lying next to him. She thought he was probably drunk.

The fisherman struggled with the rod, using both hands. His muscles bulged. But then suddenly the line reeled in very easily, as if the fish just gave up.

"You caught a boot!" exclaimed Angeline. A boot covered with seaweed hung at the end of his line.

The fisherman laughed. His laugh was high and raspy, too. He pulled in the boot and set it next to his foot. "Looks like my size," he said. He took a drink from the whiskey bottle. "Maybe I can catch the other one. Do you have a sock I can use for bait?"

"I lost my socks," said Angeline, even though she knew he was joking. "And my sneakers too. Maybe you can catch those." She laughed.

The fisherman looked at Angeline's bare feet. "Too small," he said. "I would have to throw them back." He took a long drink of beer and burped.

"What's your name?" Angeline asked him.

He grinned, looking very glad that she'd asked him that. "Oh, I got a good name," he said proudly. He said it like his name was the best thing he had, maybe the only good thing. "Cool Breezer," he told her.

"Cool Breezer," Angeline repeated. "That is a good name."

He told her how he got it. When he was in

high school, he owned a car that had no back to it. There was no rear window, no backseat, not even a trunk. "A lot of cool breezes used to blow through that car," he said. Both he and his car were each called "Cool Breezer." If someone said "Where's Cool Breezer?" you didn't know if they were talking about him or his car. Sometimes even he'd say it himself—"Where's Cool Breezer?"— and you still didn't know if he was talking about his car or himself.

He tilted his head back and poured the rest of a beer can down his throat, and also some down his shirt. He burped again. "What's your name?" he asked.

Angeline looked down at her bare feet. "Cool Feet!" she announced.

Cool Breezer laughed. He tipped his dirty wool cap very gentlemanly-like and said, "Miss Feet." He thought she had the prettiest feet he'd ever seen.

Angeline pretended to tip her imaginary cap, too, and said, "Mr. Breezer." They both laughed. "My father drives a garbage truck," she added.

"No kiddin'," laughed Cool Breezer. However, suddenly he felt very sad and empty inside. He felt envious of Mr. Feet, Cool Feet's father, who drove a garbage truck. She had spoken of him like he was a hero. He suddenly wished he had a daughter, too, like her, with pretty feet, who would be just as proud of him. All his life, he had wanted to be a hero. "What happened?" he wondered. "Where's Cool Breezer?"

"Why do you fish off the side of the pier?" Angeline asked him. "Why don't you fish off the end?"

"Well," he said, glad that she asked him a question that he could answer, "if I fished off the end of the pier, the current would take the line under the pier. That's bad. Here at the side of the pier, the current takes the line away from the pier."

"Oh," said Angeline. "Well, I'm going down to the end of the pier." She took a couple of steps, turned, and said, "So long, Cool Breezer."

Cool Breezer tipped his cap. "Cool Feet."

She walked to the end of the pier, careful not to step on any fish heads or hooks, and she tried not to get any splinters in her feet.

She sat down at the end of the pier and dangled her legs over the edge. It was about a fifteen- or twenty-foot drop to the ocean. And everywhere she looked, it went on forever.

There were millions of different kinds of fish, thousands of which nobody had even heard of. There were "Gardens of Eels" that covered acres of the ocean floor. There were caves and mountains and valleys, most of which were still a secret.

It was a great, unexplored mystery. Octopuses, sharks, bat rays, sea horses, bumphead hogfish, long-snouted hawkfish, fat innkeepers—the ocean covered more than two-thirds of the Earth's surface. Great pods of whales could swim around unnoticed, dolphins, angelfish, rainbow fish, clown fish, boots and sneakers.

Her hands gripped the pier as she ducked her head under the wooden railing. Moonfish, goosefish, flashlight fish, barracudas, she took several long deep breaths. Stonefish, lobsters, paddlefish, glass catfish, her muscles tightened. Tigerfish, scissors-tail fish, the water rocked beneath her.

She held her breath and pushed herself off the pier. She fell through the air and splashed into the salt water.

After she hit the water, she continued to fall, somersaulting as she went down. It felt like the different parts of her body were doing somersaults separately, her head, her feet, her wrists, as she kept sinking.

She had no idea how deep she'd fallen, but she was out of breath and had to hurry back to the surface to get some air. She felt a terrible pain all over from having hit the water so hard. She struggled wildly to get her head up. The water swirled all around her, splashing off the beams of the pier. She flailed her arms and legs as she tried to stay up just long enough to catch her breath, but she felt herself being pulled down again.

Her eyes burned, and her nose and throat. Surprisingly, she didn't feel cold except for her ears. Her ears were freezing. They were so cold they felt like they were going to break off.

She raised her head just enough above the surface to get another breath. Her arms and legs began to weaken. She kept swallowing water. She wanted to get air, but before she could breathe some in, she first had to cough the water out of her lungs. And as she coughed she kept taking in more water. She felt like she'd never catch up. She felt that if she could just get her breath once, she'd be all right.

She went down. She fought her way back up, coughed, gasped some air between coughs, and went down again. Her head was spinning. Her nose burned and her ears were frozen. She struggled to just get her mouth above water. She tried to take a breath but her mouth filled with water instead. She spit out as much as she could. Her eyes were on fire. She went under.

Puff-fish, turkey fish, monkeyface blenny . . .

# NINETEEN

# The Only Way to Find Her
# Is to Tell Her a Joke

"Don't hug me until I take a shower," said Abel as he headed straight for the bathroom. "Ang-e-lini," he added gleefully.

He was eagerly and anxiously looking forward to seeing Mr. Bone. He felt like a teenager about to go out on his first date. He turned on the shower and washed the banana peels out of his hair, feeling so excited that he sang, sort of:

*"Oh, I went downtown for to see my gal,*
*Sing pol-ly wol-ly doo-dle all the day.*
*We had us a time, and how,*
*Sing pol-ly wol-ly doo-dle all the day."*

He made up the words as he went along.

*"Her name's Me-lis-sa, but they call her Mis-tah,*
*Sing pol-ly wol-ly doo-dle all the day."*

He couldn't stay on tune either.

*"Fare thee well,*
*Fare well,*
*Fare well to the garbage truck.*
*Oh I'm off to Lou-si-an-a for to see my*
*Su-sy-a-na,*
*Singin' pol-ly wol-ly doo-dle like a duck."*

But he was happy.

He stopped singing as he let the shower spray his face. It had been over five years. Over five years since Nina died, since she drowned at Mitchell Beach. "That's long enough!" he decided. Now it was time for him to start having some fun. "I should go back to the beach, too," he thought. "I should take Angeline."

*"Oh I had a dog that said me-ow,*
*Sing pol-ly wol-ly doo-dle all the day.*
*So, I got a cat that said bow-wow,*
*Sing pol-ly wol-ly doo-dle all the day."*

He washed his feet and in-between his toes. He washed behind his ears four times. He washed behind his knees. He couldn't remember the last time he had washed the back of his knees.

*"Fare thee well,*
*Fare well,*
*Fare well my dar-lin' tru-u-ue . . .*
*Oh I'm off to Lou-si-an-a wid a head full o'*
    *ba-na-nas,*
*Singin' pol-ly wol-ly doo-dle doo-dle doo-oo."*

He turned off all the hot water, leaving just the cold. He stayed under it as long as he could, then stepped out of the shower and vigorously dried himself off. "Angelini!" he called. "Guess what? Gus is coming over tonight. He'll have dinner with you. Just you and Gus, Angelini!

"Do you want to know where I'll be?" he called. "Angelini? Angelooni?"

He lathered his face with shaving cream. "I've got a date!" He waited for her to respond. "I have a date, Angelooni!" He was so excited he cut himself shaving.

He went into his bedroom to get dressed. "Do you want to know with whom?" he called. "You'll never guess whom I'll be going out with tonight!" He walked out into the living room. "Do you want to guess?"

She wasn't in the living room or in the kitchen. "Where are you, Angelooni?" he called. He looked for her in all the usual hiding places, under the bed, in the closet, although he knew, with Angeline, there were no *usual* hiding places. "I haven't got time for this!" he called. "I have a date!" He decided to break the news. That would surely get her to reveal herself.

"With Mr. Bone!"

He waited. She still didn't respond. He knew Angeline was great at playing hide-and-seek. It suddenly occurred to him that it had been a long time since they had played. He wondered why that was. "I've got a date with Mr. Bone, Angelooni!"

He looked for her all over the apartment. It was a small apartment but he knew she always found a new place to hide, one that he would never think of. Once, he remembered, she sat on top of the refrigerator, right out in the open, but he was so busy looking behind things and under things that he didn't see her. If she hadn't laughed when he looked inside the mustard jar, he never would have found her.

The bell rang. He wondered if it was Angeline. He wondered what she was doing outside. He buzzed open the front door to the building and waited. It was Gus.

"Where's Angelini?" Gus asked.

"I don't know."

"Is she home?"

"She's just hiding. Angelini, Gus is here."

"Then I'll find her," said Gus. "I happen to be the world's greatest hide-and-go-seeker. Look out, Angelini! I'm gonna getcha!"

"You have to search everywhere twice," said Abel. "She watches you and waits until you've already looked in one hiding place, and then she hides there." He bent down and looked under the sofa.

"She couldn't even fit under there," said Gus.

"You don't know," said Abel. "She can fit anywhere."

While Gus searched the apartment, Abel sat on the sofa and proceeded to tell a story. "Once upon a time, there was a little girl who was left all alone in a great big house. Suddenly she hears a very faint noise . . . rap . . . rap . . . rap."

"What are you doing?" asked Gus. "Why don't you help me look for her?"

"You're not going to be able to find her that way," Abel explained. "The only way to find her is to tell her a joke."

"How do you know she can even hear you?" Gus asked.

"Oh, I'm sure she's real close," said Abel. "You don't know her like I do. She's probably on the verge of hysterical laughter." He continued with the story. "So, Angelini, the girl walks down the hallway and the noise gets louder . . . rap! . . . rap! . . . rap! And she walks into the room at the end of the hall where the noise is even louder . . . RAP . . . RAP . . . RAP. And she opens the closet door and it is even louder . . . RAP! . . . RAP! . . . RAP! And she looks into the closet and what do you think she sees?"

"What?" asked Gus.

"What do you think she saw, Angelooni?" Abel asked.

They waited.

"Wrapping paper!" Abel announced.

They waited. Angeline didn't laugh.

"That was a pretty good joke," said Gus. "I'm glad to see that. You're telling her jokes and playing with her and calling her Angelooni. You never used to do that."

Abel thought a moment. "You're right," he said. "I didn't even realize."

"And you're going out tonight, too," Gus added. "I bet that's why. See? That's what I've been trying to tell you all along."

Abel smiled. "Yeah," he said. He realized Gus was right. For the first time in a very long while, he felt like he could talk to Angeline. He wasn't afraid of her, or worried about her anymore.

## TWENTY
# Spoon and Prune

When Melissa arrived for her date with Abel, she found him and Gus each drinking a glass of salt water. "Now I know where Angeline picked up that habit," she said.

"No, really," Abel protested. "This is the first time I ever drank it. We wanted to see why Angeline liked it so much."

"And?" asked Melissa.

Abel laughed. "It's awful."

"I'm Gus," said Gus as he held out his hand. "You must be Mr. Bone."

She shook his hand. "Melissa," she said. "Where's Angeline?"

Abel and Gus looked at each other. "She's hiding," Abel said.

"Oh, I hope she's not upset because we're going out tonight," said Melissa.

"I don't think so," said Abel.

"What did she say when you told her?" Melissa asked him.

"Nothing. I mean I couldn't find her. She was already hiding."

"When was the last time you saw her?" asked Melissa.

"She was here when I came home," said Abel. "She was lying on the floor reading a book."

"That's good," said Melissa. "I was afraid something might have happened in Mrs. Hardlick's class."

"I think," Abel muttered. "I don't—she's a great hider. She's in the apartment somewhere." He didn't sound so sure anymore.

"Have you tried the aquarium?" asked Melissa.

Abel called the aquarium. "Angeline Persopolis," he told them. "She's eight years old, has black hair and green eyes." He hung up the phone. "They know who she is," he informed Gus and Melissa, "but they haven't seen her today."

"She'll be all right," Melissa assured him.

Abel wasn't worried, but that's not what he said. It was as if someone else spoke for him, someone who was eight years old, with black hair and green eyes. "You never know," he said.

"Gary!" declared Gus. "She said she had a friend named Gary. How about calling him?"

"I don't know his number," said Abel, "or his last name."

"Boone," said Melissa. "I know Gary." She smiled. "Gary Boone."

Gus laughed. "Mr. Boone," he said.

Abel looked through the phone book. "There are over two pages of Boones in here," he said. "I can't call them all."

"Wait," said Melissa. "I met his parents. What were their names? Oh . . ." She put her hands to her ears and shook her head, as if she were trying to shake their names out, like a gum ball from a gum ball machine.

"You'll just have to call up every Mr. Boone!" laughed Gus. Neither Abel nor Melissa knew why he was laughing, but he thought it was very funny that Angeline's two friends were named Mr. Bone and Mr. Boone.

Melissa hit her head. A name came out.

"Spencer," she said. And another. "Prentice. Spencer and Prentice Boone. Give me the number. I'll call them."

Gary answered the phone.

"Hello, Gary," said Melissa. "This is . . ." She paused. ". . . Mr. Bone." She explained the situation to him and asked him if he'd seen Angeline or knew where she was. He said he didn't.

"Have you tried the aquarium?" he suggested.

"She's not there," she told him.

Gary asked her what she was doing at Angeline's apartment. She told him she was planning to have dinner with Angeline's father.

"With Angeline and her father?" Gary asked.

"No, just her father."

"You mean like a date?" Gary asked.

"I guess," said his teacher.

"You're going on a date with Angeline's father!"

"Just cool it," she replied.

"Does Angeline know?"

"I don't know."

She hung up the phone. "He's coming over," she told Abel and Gus, "to help look for her."

That was one reason. The other reason why

he was coming over was because he wanted to see what Mr. Bone looked like when she went out on a date. He also wanted to be there when Angeline found out her father was going on a date with Mr. Bone, and hopefully he'd be the one who would tell her.

When Gary arrived, all four of them searched the apartment.

"You check that side of the bed, Mr. Boone," said Gus, "while I check this side. That way she can't switch back and forth."

Gary laughed. "Okay, Gus," he said.

Abel tried to organize the search very systematically. He locked the bathroom door so she couldn't circle around them.

"You sure look pretty tonight, Mr. Bone," said Gary.

"Thank you, Gary," she said.

"Do you always look so pretty when you go out on dates?" he asked.

"Knock it off, Gary," she replied.

"Don't you think she looks pretty, Mr. Persopolis?" he asked Angeline's father.

Abel blushed. Fortunately, just as he opened his mouth, the phone rang, with perfect saved-by-the-bell timing. It made everyone laugh.

Abel answered it.

"Yes, I'm her father," he said. "Yes. Yes."

Melissa watched as he slowly turned pale. His whole body began to tremble. The sight of him made her feel like crying.

Abel dropped the phone. It dangled on the cord. He walked slowly across the room. His face quivered.

Gary felt like crying, too. He now wished he had never come over. He held Miss Turbone's hand.

Abel opened his mouth, but all he was able to say was "Mitchell Beach," as he tried to fight back his tears.

## TWENTY-ONE
# Pretty Feet and Green Her Eyes

Gary squeezed Mr. Bone's hand. He waited for Angeline's father to say more, only he didn't think he wanted to hear it.

Abel's face was now streaked with tears. "Hospital," he whispered.

"Let's go," said Melissa, still holding Gary's hand. "I'll drive."

They rode the elevator down to the street and climbed into her car. She and Abel got in the front and Gary and Gus sat in the back. And on the very rear of the car was a bumper sticker which said SAVE THE WHALES.

"She fell off Mitchell Pier," Abel uttered. He stared out the window at a billboard advertising chewing gum as if he were suddenly very interested in which brand packed the most punch.

Gary was glad he got to go along. He thought that if anybody had stopped to think about it, they wouldn't have brought him. Kids never get to go along on emergencies. They would have sent him home, instead. He felt terrible for feeling glad about this. He didn't think he should be feeling glad about anything, when—and this suddenly occurred to him—when Angeline might be dead.

He tried to think about something else, or better yet, not to think at all. He wondered why he was thinking so much. His brain was going a mile a minute. He didn't think he usually thought so much.

He wondered if Mr. Bone and Gus were thinking as much as he was, or if he was the only one, because he was a goon.

He didn't wonder about what Angeline's father was thinking. He didn't want to think about that.

When they got to the hospital, they were directed to a waiting room where they were told to wait. There was somebody else already in the room, but he looked more like a patient than a visitor. He was dressed in a hospital gown and robe. Gary wondered who he was.

He suddenly thought of a joke. "If we have to wait, does that mean we are waiters, like we have to serve food?" Then he felt awful for having thought of it. "How could I make up jokes, *now*?" he wondered.

"Gary," said Mr. Bone. She held out a tissue to him.

He took the tissue from her. He hadn't realized he'd been crying. "Angeline would have thought it was a funny joke," he thought.

The man in the hospital gown shivered.

A doctor finally walked in. "Are you Angeline's parents?" he asked.

"I'm her father," said Abel.

The doctor took a deep breath. "Angeline was underwater a long time, I'm afraid," he said, "before Mr., um—" He gestured toward the man wearing the hospital gown and robe. "Mr., um—" He pointed again at the man.

The man shivered. "Cool Breezer," he said in a high and raspy voice.

"Before Mr. Cool Breezer was able to pull her out," said the doctor.

Everyone turned and looked at Cool Breezer. Cool Breezer looked away.

"When she arrived, her lungs were almost completely filled with salt water," the doctor said. "We've done all we can do. Now it's up to her."

Melissa put her arm around Abel. "She'll make it," she said. "I know she will."

"Angelini's tough," said Gus.

"I'll take you to see her now," said the doctor. "But before I do, I want to prepare you. She won't be able to see or hear you. I think the earliest we can expect any kind of positive reaction from her won't be for at least another twenty-four hours."

"Then will she—" Abel started to ask.

"Her brain went a long time without oxygen," said the doctor. "You just never know." He led them down a long corridor, through several sets of double doors.

"You never know," Abel repeated.

He led them into Angeline's room, then left. Angeline lay on top of a bed, not under the covers. She was wearing a hospital gown, like the one Cool Breezer was wearing. There were bottles hanging above her, and there were tubes coming out of the bottles and sticking into her arms and neck.

A nurse was stationed alongside her. The nurse stood up and moved out of the way as Abel approached.

Abel silently stared at his daughter. "Mitchell Beach," he said after a while. He looked around the room. "What was she doing at Mitchell Beach?"

Cool Breezer shrugged.

"Nina," muttered Abel. "Her mother drowned at Mitchell Beach. I haven't been back there since." He looked back at Angeline. "What were you doing there, Angel Face?" he asked. He didn't know why he had just called her that. He'd never called her Angel Face before. Nina used to call her that.

Gary thought that he understood, sort of, why Angeline went to the beach, but he couldn't explain it. "Mr. Bone, may I have another tissue please?" he asked.

She gave him one.

"Cool Breezer?" said Gus. "What—"

Cool Breezer violently shivered, interrupting him. "May I have a tissue, Mr. Bone?" He didn't seem to think that she had a strange name.

She gave him a tissue and he blew his nose.

Then he told them what had happened. "I was fishing off Mitchell Pier," he said in his scratchy voice. "Cool Feet—I mean, Angeline walked up to me, and we talked, and—"

"Wha'd she say?" Abel asked. "Do you remember what she said?"

Cool Breezer thought a moment. "She said you drove a garbage truck."

Cool Breezer had rebaited his hook after he caught the boot. He had dropped the line back in the water, sat down, and opened a new can of beer. He hummed to himself and looked around for Cool Feet. He stood up. He didn't see her.

He threw his beer down and ran to the end of the pier. He looked over the rail and saw her being washed underneath it. The next thing he knew he was underwater.

He hadn't taken off his shoes until after he was in the water. He swam after her and managed to grab her by the shirt. He wrapped his arm around her waist and struggled to get her back to shore. The tide was pulling them out while the waves kept knocking them forward. He tried his best to hold her above the water as he kept being swept under.

At last he was able to feel the ground with his tiptoes, but was unable to make any progress until a giant wave crashed directly on top of them. They tumbled in with the white water.

He carried her onto the sand. Her face was covered with sand and her mouth was filled with salt water. He tried giving her mouth-to-mouth resuscitation but she didn't respond, so he picked her up and ran in his wet socks across the beach to the liquor store on the other side of the street.

"Howdy, Cool Breezer," the man behind the counter said. "You look like you need some brew. Who's your little friend?"

"Call an ambulance," Cool Breezer said, then collapsed on the floor.

"I'm sorry," he said when he finished telling them what had happened.

"You have nothing to be sorry for," said Melissa. "You saved her life. You're a hero."

He had always wanted to be a hero. He thought about what he had done and he realized it did sound like something a hero would do. Still, as he looked at Angeline lying there, he didn't feel like a hero. "I'm sorry," he repeated. He looked at her feet sticking out from under her hospital gown. They were still the prettiest feet he'd ever seen. "Cool Feet," he said sadly.

Abel bent over and kissed Angeline on the cheek. "Someday, Angeline," he whispered.

Melissa held Abel's hand.

"She was all I ever lived for," Abel told her. "All I ever cared about. I was always so afraid I'd blow it for her. Well, Abel," he said, "you finally did it."

"No," cried Melissa. "It wasn't your fault. You mustn't believe that."

Gus and Gary walked up to Angeline. Gus kissed her on the cheek. "Angelini," he said. He too was crying.

Gary also kissed her. He wanted to rip all the tubes out of her. It seemed to him that the tubes were sucking life out of her, instead of giving it to her. "I heard a new joke," he whispered. "You want to hear my joke, Angeline? Why doesn't an elephant need a suitcase?"

"Why?" Angeline whispered.

Gary's mouth dropped open. He couldn't speak. All he could do was point, loudly.

"I give up. Why?" Angeline asked again.

Why wouldn't he answer her? He just stood there, looking like a goon. She looked around the room and tried to figure out where she was, but it was too crazy to figure out. Nothing made any sense. Why was Cool Breezer jumping up and down and whooping and shrieking, she wondered. And why was he dressed so funny? What happened to his wool cap? Why did he just kiss her foot? And now the other one!

"Stop that!" she laughed. "What's going on here?"

And who was that lady dressed in white coming toward her and shouting, "Doctor! Doctor!"

"Why doesn't an elephant need a suitcase?" she asked. Why wouldn't anybody answer her?

The lady in white shrugged. "Because it never takes a trip? Because it doesn't own any clothes? Doctor!"

That's not even funny, she thought. "That's not a joke!" she shouted. Why was everybody laughing? It wasn't even funny. She saw her father, and Gus, and Mr. Bone. Were they laughing or crying? She was getting very angry.

"What's going on here?" she demanded, but the madder she got, the more she yelled, the crazier everyone acted. What were these tubes sticking in her? Why was Gus carrying Gary around on his shoulders?

"Are you all crazy?" she screamed. Wouldn't someone tell her what was happening. "Cool Breezer?" she pleaded, but all he did was yell and scream. And Gary was unable to talk.

"Doctor!" the lady in white shouted. Why did she want a doctor? She looked too happy to be sick.

And why—and this was what really didn't make any sense at all—why were her father and Mr. Bone . . . kissing???

## TWENTY-TWO
# You Never Know

High on the cliffs above the secret cove, the weary sailor and the one-eyed pirate dueled to the death. Tied to a tree, the beautiful lady didn't make a sound for fear of waking up the drunken crew. The sailor thrust his sword through the pirate's evil heart. The pirate raised his sword in a menacing manner, tottered on the edge of the cliff, then fell to his watery grave.

The garbage truck, clean and bright and shiny like a fire engine, pulled up in front of the apartment building and parked. Gus rode the elevator up to the fourth floor.

"C'mon, Angelooni, let's go," Abel called into the bathroom. "Gus is here."

"Just a sec," said Angeline.

Abel and Gus waited for her, sillily grinning at each other.

Oh so quietly, the sailor tiptoed through the sleeping crew and untied the beautiful lady. And for the first time, he kissed her sweet lips. They gathered up the gold and the jewels and sailed off to San Francisco, where they lived happily ever after.

Angeline stepped out of the bathroom, wearing her best dress. "Let's go," she said.

"Well, don't you look pretty," said Gus.

Abel and Gus rode the elevator down as Angeline raced it down the stairs. All out of breath, she beat it by half a second but she pretended she had been waiting there for hours. "Well, it's about time," she said, looking at an imaginary watch. "What took you so long?"

"We stopped for a hamburger and french fries," said Gus.

Angeline laughed. She ran outside to look at the truck. It was so big. It had a huge hood. And its wheels were almost as big as she was. She studied the contraption in the back. It was the place where you dumped the garbage. It was a long flat box without a top. You dump the garbage in it; then, from inside the truck, you pull a lever that raises it over the top of the truck; then you push a button, and it turns over.

Gus opened the door and Angeline climbed into the cab. She sat in the middle. Abel drove and Gus sat on the other side of her. She laughed with delight as her father revved the motor. Gus reached across her and tooted the horn. They were off.

Angeline had been down the same streets many times before. She had seen the same billboards, parking lots, and gas stations. But somehow, looking at them now from inside the garbage truck made them seem special, almost magical. "Where to first?" she asked.

"We still have to pick up Mr. Boone and Mr. Bone," said Gus.

Angeline laughed. It was the first time she had heard his joke. She thought it was the funniest joke Gus had ever told, a lot funnier than the tomatoes.

They picked up Mr. Bone first, at her condominium. She was waiting outside and waved enthusiastically as the truck drove up. Unlike Angeline, she was wearing her old clothes. She wore torn blue jeans with patches and she carried a picnic basket.

Abel stepped out of the truck and took the basket from her.

"Hello, Gus, Angeline," she said and quickly kissed Abel. She climbed inside.

She took Angeline's spot in the middle, and Angeline sat on Gus's lap. Abel handed the picnic basket back to Melissa. Angeline showed her around. "This is the lever that works the thing in back, and this one, here, this one dumps out the whole truck, like when you're at the garbage dump." She turned to her father. "Are we going to the dump?" she asked. "Could we go there too, please? Please?"

Abel shook his head. "Sorry, but we don't have any garbage," he told her. "They won't let you in the dump without garbage."

"Shucks!" said Angeline. "We should have brought some from home. Maybe Gary's family has some garbage that they don't want."

They pulled up in front of Gary's house. Angeline ran out and got him. They raced back to the truck.

Abel tried to figure out the best seating arrangement for the five of them.

"Gary and I could sit in the thing in back," suggested Angeline.

"Ooh, that sounds like fun," said Gary.

"I'll sit back there with them," said Gus. "Just don't turn us over."

Gus, Gary, and Angeline climbed into the contraption in the back. From inside the truck, Abel slowly raised them into the air. "Whoa," said Gary and Angeline together. They had a good view in all directions.

Mostly, the truck followed the regular Thursday route, but Abel also combined some of the best parts from the other days of the week as well. They went past the bowling alley, the giant donut sign, the police department, city hall, and the miniature golf course. As for the regular Thursday customers, they were just out of luck.

Angeline angrily punched herself in the leg.

"What's the matter, Angelini?" Gus asked.

"We forgot to ask Gary if he had any garbage," she said.

Gus laughed.

"Now we can't go to the dump!" she complained.

"Oh, yeah, that's too bad," said Gary. "We got lots of garbage that we don't want." Then he giggled and said "Angelini," the way he heard Gus say it.

They went past the automobile dealership, the car wash, and the ravioli factory.

"Look, the ravioli factory!" Angeline pointed out. "Do you get lots of garbage from there, Gus?"

Gus smiled. "Oh, yeah, they are one of our best clients."

"That's neat that Mr. Bone came too," said Gary. "I didn't think my folks would let me come and miss school, but she's a teacher! Imagine, a teacher missing school to ride in a garbage truck."

"Well, you want to know what I think, Gary?" Gus asked slyly. "I think Angeline's father and Mr. Bone are falling in love."

Gary and Angeline giggled, and Gus giggled too.

They passed the Mexican restaurant and the paint store. "You missed it," Angeline told Gary. "When we picked up Mr. Bone, she kissed my father. On the lips!"

"I saw them kiss at the hospital," said Gary. "Remember?"

"That's right," said Angeline.

"Did Gary tell you that he kissed you at the hospital?" Gus asked. "When you were unconscious?"

"Yech!" said Angeline.

Gary denied it. "I did not!"

They passed the radio station and a condemned building.

"Maybe your father and Mr. Bone will get married," said Gary. "Then Mr. Bone will be your mother, instead of just your teacher."

Angeline laughed with delight. "And then if we get married too," she said, "she'll also be *your* mother!"

Past the sweater and socks store, where they give you a matching pair of socks with every sweater you buy.

"Then you'll grow up to be a world-famous oceanographer," said Gary.

"Or a garbageperson," said Angeline. "And you'll be a world-famous comedian!"

"Or a garbageperson," said Gary.

Then, for a special surprise, the truck headed up the road to the dump.

"Boy, wouldn't that be something if that all really happens?" said Gary. "Someday, Angeline?"

Angeline gazed out across the garbage dump. She had a gleam in her eye as she said, "You never know."

And slapped across the back of the garbage truck, there was a bumper sticker that said SAVE THE WHALES.

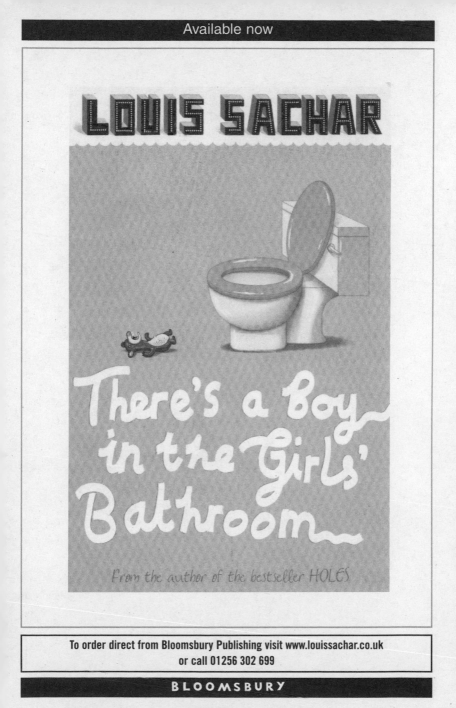

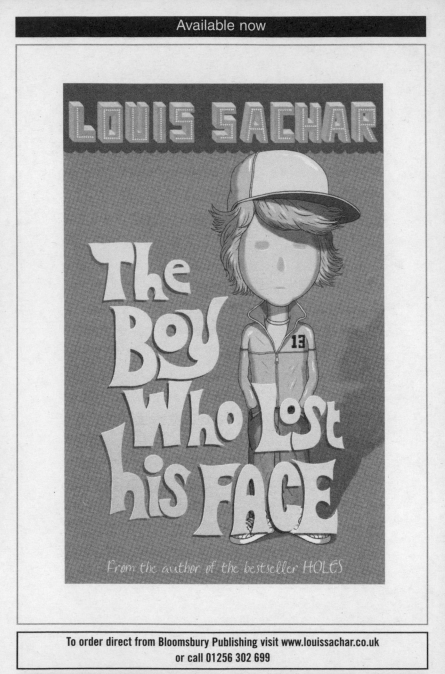